D0034271

Contents

This book is dedicated to all who lost their freedom or their lives in the holocaust of the Atlantic slave trade, called the Ma'afa, in Africa.

> Songs we would never hear! Histories we would never know! Art we would never see! Because the European had the capacity to destroy and didn't have the moral restraint not to. (Maulana Karenga)

It is also dedicated to my dear friend Kwame Dabbisah of Ghana, who first told me the story of the sorceress who saved her people from slavery.

But most of all, it is dedicated to the life of Malcolm Boyd (1971–2018), the Pied Piper of Uralla. Somunye, my brother—we are one.

Acknowledgements

Thanks for the help of many good friends, including Rochelle England, Malcolm Boyd, Virginia Barry, Cheryl Benn, and Jenene Heath, who let me read the evolving book to them, bounce ideas off them, and helped with editing and research. I was also assisted by my excellent cover designer and formatter Georgi Mikaylov, my indefatigable copy editor Elaine Roughton, my awesome fiction coach R. E. Vance, and the many staff and friends at www.self-publishingschool.com. It is a better book because of their help.

(from L'Homme de le Terre by Elisee Reclus 1896)

She will always carry on
Something is lost, something is found
They will keep on speaking her name
Some things change, some stay the same . . .

Hymn to Her by Meg Keene, 1986

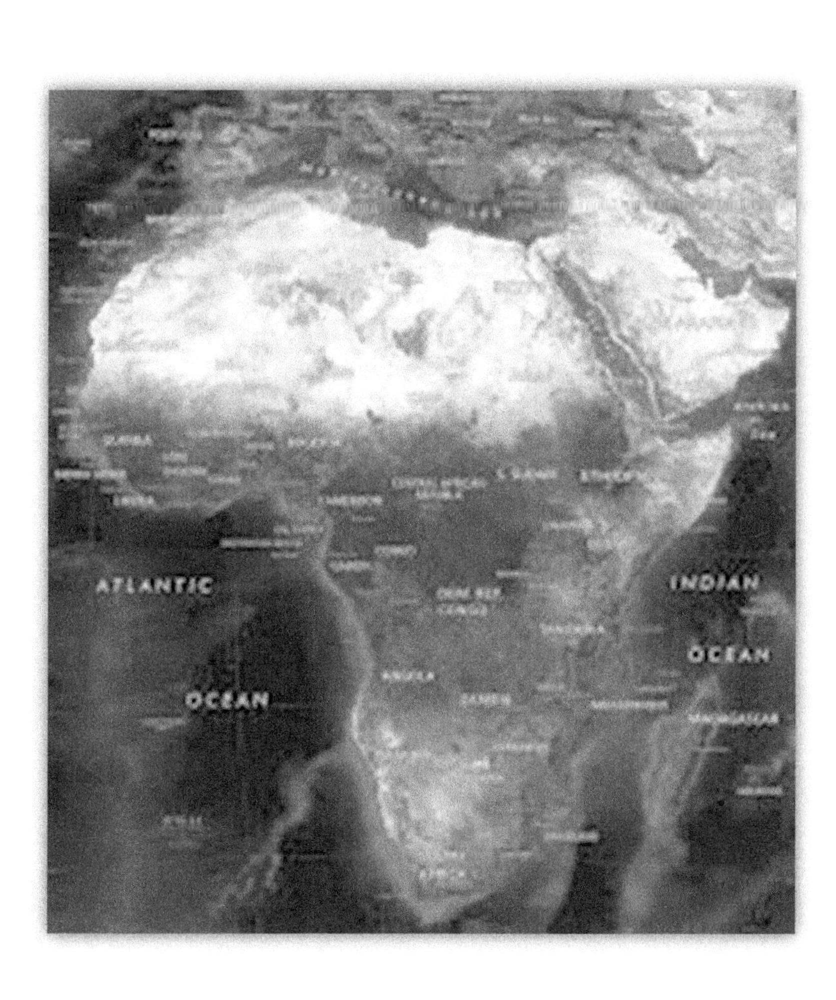
ATLANTIC
OCEAN
INDIAN
OCEAN

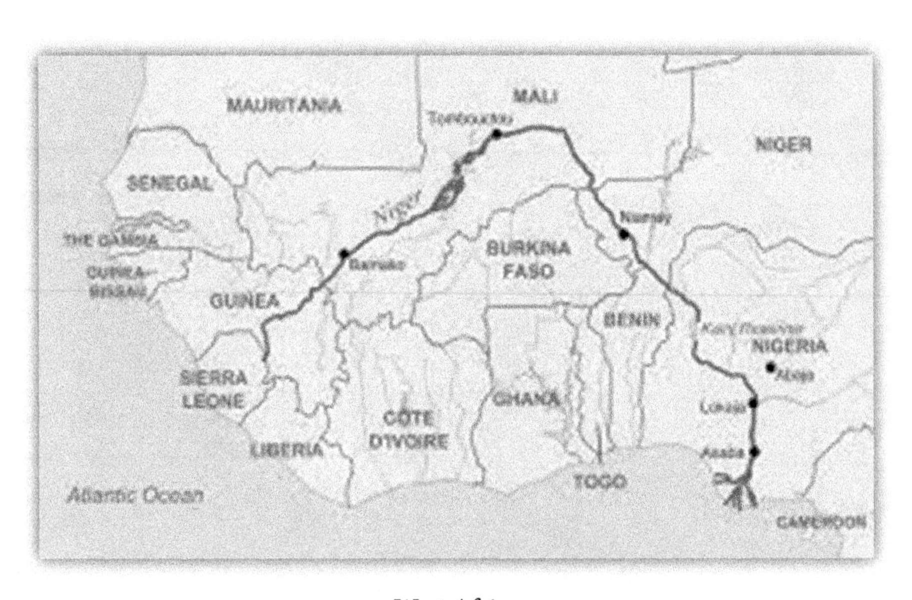
MAURITANIA
MALI
NIGER
SENEGAL
THE GAMBIA
GUINEA
SIERRA
LEONE
LIBERIA
CÔTE
D'IVOIRE
BURKINA
FASO
GHANA
TOGO
BENIN
NIGERIA
Niger
Atlantic Ocean

West Africa

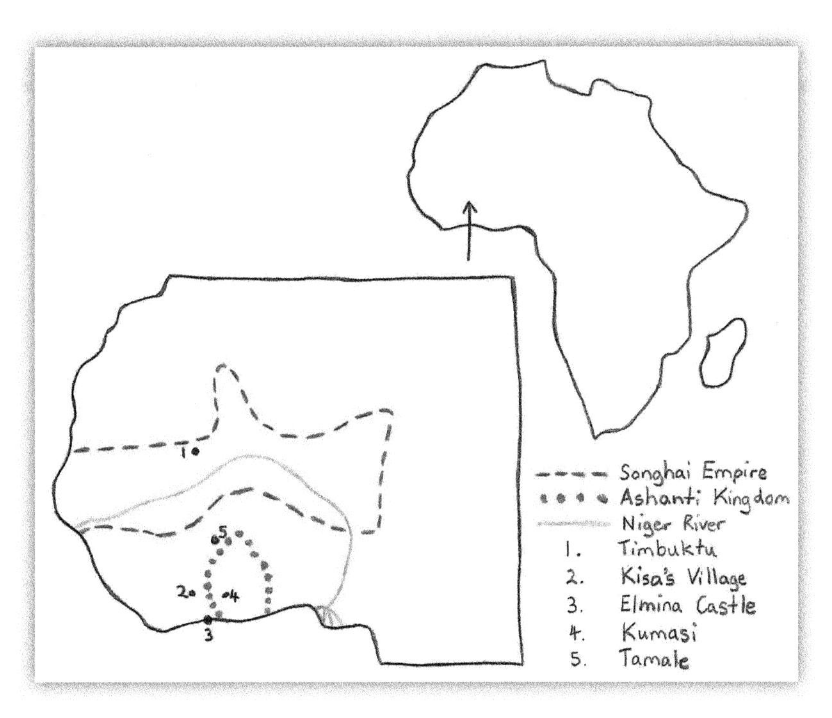

Kisa's village

Prologue

Father never let the story be told without following the proper rituals. After the evening meal, he made an offering of palm wine on the sacred stone at the head of the firepit, and then he built a large fire. The village fetish priest put on his feathers and danced away the evil spirits. At last, Grandmother walked out and took her seat near the stone. We sat around her in the fire's warmth while she told the story of our ancestor, the great prophetess who fought to save our tribe from the slave masters.

She always began with prayers, to Nyame the creator and to the goddess Asase Ya, embodied in our Mother Africa:

'Mother, sing me a song. A song that will ease our pain, mend broken bones, bring wholeness again. A song that will catch our babies when they are born, sing our death songs, teach us how to mourn. Show us the medicine of the healing herbs, the value of the holy spirit. Mother, heal our hearts that we may serve you, for you are the Tree of Life for us.'

Then, in soft words, she told us the story of the mother of our nation, Kisa, the greatest sorceress who had ever lived, and how she saved our tribe three hundred years ago.

'Many tribes disappeared in the terrible time of the slave forts,' she began. 'The people did not fight back, and the price for slaves was so great that the slave masters took everyone. Only those that hid or became part of the evil survived. We were among those who chose to hide and then, because of Kisa, to fight back.

'The tribes most in danger were those closest to the white devils' forts, where they bought the people and sent them to the land across the sea. We were only a day's walk from the great slave castle Elmina. We could have disappeared across the sea with the rest, but for the sorceress . . .'

A hush fell over us as she continued.

'She was the mother of our nation, but she began life as a child, as do we all . . .'

PART 1

1619-1630

CHAPTER 1

The Sentinel Tree

'Higher, higher!' The taunts followed her up the tree, but she ignored them. She was going to the top without their help. At three years old, she was as light as a feather, and her hands and feet had a fearsome grip when life depended on it.

Higher she climbed up the swaying branches of the half-dead giant. She climbed above the peaked thatch roofs of the village huts, above the surrounding forest until she could see to the ends of her world. In every direction, the forest went on forever, covering the lines of hills as far as she could see.

The world's wind was strong up here and whipped through her curly hair. It swayed the branches to and fro, and she heard one crack. She felt invincible, one with the gods of earth and air and fire.

She looked above her and stared at the great black spear that was the top of the lightning-struck old tree. This was why she had climbed so high through the living part of the tree—to see it and touch it.

For half its height, the tree branched out into many leafy green branches snaking out in all directions—a tree of life covered this time of year in small but beautiful creamy-white flowers. But above that, the tree was dead, all branches blown away by the force and flames of the lightning strike.

Kisa was standing on the highest leafy branch and clinging to the base of the great black spear that dwarfed her in its size, and rose so high that she imagined it touched the sky. She longed to climb further, but it was too smooth—hardened to steel by the lightning the night that the old great-grandmother rode on the wings of the owl to find it.

She imagined it all: the desperate journey to find a safe place for her people, the great storm rising till Great-Grandmother thought she would drown, then the lightning coming from the sky god himself to show her the tree that would lead them to safety . . .

Suddenly, the sound of the wind in the leaves turned to words. 'Akwaaba,' the tree whispered to her. 'Welcome.'

'You speak!' the child said, forgetting to answer the greeting politely. She felt welcomed and protected.

The leaves whispered back to her, but she could not understand it.

'Come down now, child!' Grandmother's voice rang out from below. It allowed for no argument. She made her way slowly back to earth.

'I will come back, brother tree,' she whispered as she reached the lowest branch. The tree shivered as she leaped to the ground. And as she ran, she heard a deep voice echo behind her: 'You . . . Akwaaba . . . always . . .'

The laughter of the children followed her as Grandmother took her by the hand and led her back to her hut. 'Are you angry, Grandmother?' she asked as they entered.

'No, Kisa. I was proud of you. To go all the way to the top! And at your age . . . you are very clever. But it is not wise to taunt the gods for too long. They may choose to prove you are mortal and cast you back down. What did you see up there?' she asked as she sat down by the cook pot and cuddled the girl on her lap.

'Oh, Grandmother, I could see the whole world!'

The village was a collection of small round huts with wattle and daub walls and peaked, thatched roofs. For privacy and comfort, there were beautifully woven mats over the doors. The huts were not built out in the open area but were cunningly concealed among the trees within circles of ditches, brush piles, and brambles, beyond which was thick jungle on all sides. They were built around a central open area with Kisa's tree on guard at the highest point of the hill on which the village huddled.

In villages like this one, the biggest hut belonged to the chief and his family. But the best huts belonged to the spiritual leaders of the people—the fetish priests and the sorceresses known as obeah women. In this village, there was no fetish priest, the last one having disappeared in mysterious circumstances years before, so the old obeah woman that everyone called Grandmother performed all the spiritual and medical duties and rituals.

Grandmother had no children of her own, for she was the spiritual mother of the entire tribe. The people turned to the chief and the council of elders for matters of law, but they turned to Grandmother for almost everything else. She was the village midwife and doctor. She healed the sick and prepared the dead for burial. She had a virtual pharmacy of herbal remedies in her hut and knew the uses of them all.

She also carried the history and wisdom of the ages in her old mind. She was the village griot, the storyteller, who knew the stories going back for generations, and she passed this wisdom on around the campfire at night. She mediated with the gods and demons and spoke for Nyame, the supreme deity, and Asase Ya, the earth mother goddess.

Of all the village children, Kisa was the most special to her. She saw herself in the child—brave, intelligent, and burning with curiosity. A sign on the night of Kisa's birth told Grandmother that this child was her successor. A crow, a symbol of strength, came to sit on the hut, waiting for her birth. Then Grandmother had a vision of a warrior as the baby left the womb into her waiting hands, and she heard herself give the child the name Kisa.

Ama, Kisa's mother, had another name chosen, but Grandmother insisted, and Ama knew it was bad luck to cross her. Neither revealed the name for weeks as mother and baby were kept in seclusion till it was clear that she was strong enough to survive. Then a joyous naming ceremony was held, and that was the moment that Thimba, Kisa's father, saw her for the first time and carried her out of the hut for all to see, held her up for the gods to admire, and proclaimed her name to the tribe.

Three years later, Grandmother had truly seen the future in this girl: Kisa was already strong, brave, and wilful. She chuckled at the thought of the small girl sitting so high in the old tree before she called her down. Tree climbing had been Grandmother's favourite childhood activity too.

Of all the children in the village, only Kisa was allowed to follow her anywhere. Over time, the old woman had grown intolerant of the very young. They irritated her. She had too much to do to pander to small children. But Kisa was different, and the old obeah's assistants noticed that from the time she could crawl, Kisa was welcome at Grandmother's side.

Grandmother talked to Kisa like an adult. She told the child the entire story of her life and all about the obeah woman who had been her teacher. It didn't matter to her if Kisa understood everything, but she started the child's education right from the beginning.

'When I was a child, our old obeah woman took me as her apprentice and taught me everything I know. Oh, I was like you, small and wild. I loved to climb palm trees and look out over the ocean. I wish I could show you the ocean.' She sighed.

'What does it look like, Grandmother?'

'It is water. It is blue sometimes and other times grey. And it moves, always moving. It roars, and it creates the wind. It is a living thing, the ocean, and so big that it could swallow you with one wave and never notice . . . It cannot be described in words, but someday, you will see it . . .

'In the meantime'—she looked sternly at the child, who met her gaze with a look as serious—'I am going to teach you everything I know.

'I know the history of our people back to the beginning. I know where we came from, but I cannot see so far into the future. I do not know what will become of us. Times are changing and not for the better.

'From my obeah, Great-Grandmother, I learned the names and uses of the herbs and medicines of the forest and sea. I learned to heal the sick, bring children into the world, and escort the spirits of the dead to the next world.

'I learned how to make love potions and poisons too. She taught me about the spirit world and introduced me to the gods and the devils. She sent me alone into the wilderness to find my spirit animal, the owl, just as I will send you one day to find yours.

'She showed me the magic that connects us to our ancestors, to every obeah woman back to the First Woman of our people. They are there to help us when we need them. They will help you too, Kisa.'

Sometimes Grandmother talked in riddles or told stories. Kisa loved the stories of Kwaku Ananse the Spider. He was the youngest son of Nyame, the sky god, and his wife, Asase Ya, earth mother goddess, and he was a trickster who pulled pranks on other creatures.

'We had no stories until Kwaku stole them from his father, the sun god Nyame, who made the first man, Kamunu. He gave Kamunu a tongue to speak and told him to give names to all creation. But Nyame, who has all the stories, for he sees all, did not share them with Kamunu and his people.

So Kwaku stole some of them and gave them to the mothers to tell their children.'

At the end of each story, Grandmother said, 'Go home now, Kisa. Sleep time.' And Kisa went.

One of the jobs of the young girls, including Kisa, was to fetch water from the river during the dry season. When it was wet, the gardens were watered by the rain, and the villagers could get their water from the tiny rivulets that flowed off their hill. But when the dry times came, water had to be carried from the closest permanent water source, a river west of the village.

To get there was a hike of two hours and the way back took much longer, being uphill all the way and with each girl carrying a full jar of water on her head. The girls chattered most of the way down, but as they approached the river, they were hushed by their guardian, an older man or woman, who always accompanied them.

'It's not safe now. Quiet!' The guard went ahead to check that no one was around. Not far from the river ran a road where strangers might be passing. If no one was seen, the girls were allowed to bathe and play in the cool water until, as the sun started its downward path to dusk time, they were chased out of the water and made their way back up the mountain, straight-backed with the precious water jars on their heads.

When they were a long way from the road and the river, they were allowed to talk and sing. Walking songs kept the time of their steps, and stories made the hard hike easier.

The adults liked to tell them about the hyena men to scare the girls. 'Hyena man, he very handsome. Young girls, they fall in love with him. But behind his hair on back of neck, he has another mouth. You marry him, he takes you away and eats you! Never see your family again. So let your father and mother choose your husband for you. They not silly like you young girls!'

The girls were scared of the hyena men and preferred to tell stories of the trickster Kwaku Ananse, and Kisa loved them all.

'Very clever, that Kwaku. Some time he spider with man face,' one girl began.

Then a second raised eight fingers and said, 'Or man with eight legs!'

Others took turns telling his adventures, 'He cunning. Old Brother Death chase but never catch him.'

'How he do that?' Kisa asked.

Her friend Esi answered, 'He makes a web all the way to heaven. Old Brother Death, he not allowed in heaven so he not catch 'im. That how we know Kwaku is really a god. Animal cannot climb to heaven, people cannot climb to heaven, but Kwaku can, so he a god. The son of the sky god himself, Kwaku is.'

That caused an argument. 'But when he down here, he not like a god. He greedy. Want all the food—leave none for us!'

'Yes, but clever too! Lizard not catch him. Bird not get him. Remember how he tricked chameleon?'

Then someone would start chanting with hand motions, 'Chay chay Koolay', as she tapped her head. The rest of the girls answered in chorus, 'Chay chay Koolay', as they tapped their heads.

The leader chanted out the name of each girl in turn to get their attention, and the group responded each time, and all keeping the time by clapping: 'Chay chay Kisa sa . . .'

'Chay chay Kisa sa!'

'Chay chay Esi sa . . .'

'Chay chay Esi sa!'

As they neared the end of their walk, they finished with a rousing: 'Kum adende, kum adende . . . Hey!'

And so the stories and songs unfolded as their legs carried them back home. Their parents greeted them, drank thirstily, and watered their precious crops. As the sun set, they finished the trek back to the village together, to an evening's meal by the cook fires, family time with many more stories, and then to sleep.

Stories, songs, and dancing were not just for special occasions but were interwoven into every aspect of life. There were songs and stories for each activity, whether it was gardening or cooking, weaving or building huts. And whenever there were songs, someone was dancing. Life was not easy, but the songs, the stories, the drums, and the dancing all made it more enjoyable as they carried out all the daily tasks necessary for survival in the depths of the ancient forest that protected them.

CHAPTER 2

Village in a Maze

Even as a toddler, Kisa could sense that all was not well in the village. Too many times there was nothing to eat but thin porridge at dawn. Each day, the adults went to the gardens, but often they returned home empty-handed. Some days, they hid in silence, and the children were not allowed outside to play.

On those days, the fires were put out. Kisa and the other children were told in hushed voices that demons were near. They had to be quiet, or they might be captured and taken away. When the danger passed and they were allowed to play outside again, most of the games involved chasing and hiding. In this way, Kisa and the other children learned the skills they needed to hide from whatever demons should come to the village.

Once every ten days, if it was safe, the villagers gathered together around a central outdoor fire. It began with the drums calling everyone to the gathering. Softly at first and then more compellingly, the drums spoke to the people, whose feet responded. Tools were dropped, babes were strapped to backs, and food was loaded in baskets and placed on heads as the people gathered. Offerings of food and drink were placed for the gods and the rest where all could share. Children were relegated to older siblings so their parents could dance. The dancing often went on for hours.

When the drums fell silent, people sat to eat and were entertained as different men and women took turns telling stories. The men liked tales of bravery against enemies. The women told stories of relationships, how each member was related to everyone else, and what their roles were in the tribe. And they all loved to tell funny stories about each other.

'I saw Esi trip on a stone today. Do you remember the time she slipped in the mud and slid down the hill clutching her water jar?'

'Yes, but you pushed me!'

It was all in fun, and nobody minded as they laughed at each other's foibles.

When Kisa had enough of food and dancing, she climbed high into the Sentinel Tree, where she nestled in her friend's branches until it was time for the children to go to bed. Often, no one noticed her when parents sent the little ones scuttling away with their older siblings to guard them, and so she learned early about the serious business that followed the feasting.

When he had enough of gossip, Chief Abrafo spoke. He kept the people informed of village facts of life: how much food there was, whether raiders had been seen, if any trading with other villages was in the offing. This night, Chief Abrafo reported that the defences were strong and the warriors well-trained. He was expecting a good harvest with plentiful food for the year to come.

Then there followed the serious business of the village. At this time, anyone could bring up a complaint or grievance. Each side spoke, and then the people came to a decision about the issue and the consequences. When Chief Abrafo saw there was a consensus, he pronounced the verdict, and that was the end of the matter.

The last to speak was Grandmother. She had no other name that they knew. Everyone grew up calling her Grandmother even though she could not possibly have borne so many children. She was old beyond understanding, wrinkled and wizened by the weight of years, but she was lively and full of stories that she told with twinkling eyes that belied the hardship of the life she had lived.

She was the village historian, carrying the knowledge of the ancestors, knowledge of the past that defined the people. Over the years of Kisa's early life and from her vantage point in the Sentinel Tree, Kisa heard all the stories from the creation of the tribe to the present.

'Tonight, I will tell you how we came to this most secret place in all the great forest. Our ancestors were happy on the coast until the white devils came. I was not yet born then, but my teacher was a child who saw it happen.

'Once, our ancestors lived next to the ocean and were rich. They took fish from the sea and bush meat from the forest. They grew millet, cocoa, bananas, and coconuts—all the food they needed, and they never went hungry.' Grandmother sighed.

'Oh, for the taste of sweet ocean fish! I think I miss that the most,' she grumbled. 'Then the white devils came—ugly men with pale skin, strange-coloured hair hanging lank, and dirty. They were evil-smelling and wore strange clothes, and worse, they had guns and cannons, which the ancestors had never seen before.

'They built a stone tower near our village. Every day, they rang a bell, and every night, they lit candles in the tower to keep their ships from hitting the rocks. Then they built a great fort.

'At first, they traded for gold, ivory, wood, and cocoa. They brought us good iron and cloth from the north, and they brought new foods from the land across the sea: maize, sorghum, and cassava. We liked these new foods, and life seemed good.

'Then a man came to visit the trading post. He was dressed differently than the others: he was wearing a rich man's clothes. He talked to our fishermen about the land across the ocean. The fishermen call it the Middle Passage because it goes to a faraway land. Our people do not go there often, for it is a long and dangerous journey, but we know of it from those who made it and returned.

'That man went away, and the ancestors thought no more about it. But later after the slave fort was built, we learned that man, who was called Columbus, had crossed the Middle Passage and conquered the lands to the west. People now say he discovered those western lands even though our people always knew they were there. And that is where our people are now being taken to work until they die.

'In that new land, they wanted slaves—many, many slaves. There were never enough. They took so many that some tribes were wiped out. Others took advantage of the new trade, capturing people of smaller nations like ours and selling them for guns and iron, to make them strong. Some of the Fante and the Ashanti people followed this path, but we did not believe in slavery or warfare, seeking only to live in peace.

'Slavery was not new. We have known this evil for more generations than I can count. It used to be that the Nyamweri, the people of the moon, would walk out of the east, led by dusky men with great black beards. They were the sons of Arabs from the far north, the followers of the prophet of the desert. Those men mated with Swahili women, and the sons of those devils carried on their evil work, taking captives from our villages to the east to be slaves.

'When the first white devils came and built the great fort, the people of the moon and their Arab/Swahili masters began selling their captives to the devils in that fortress instead of taking them east. That is when the raids on our coastal village began. At first, they took only a few men, but it was never enough. The white devils always wanted more and more. The black ships appeared and took our people away across the Middle Passage, never to be seen again.'

A low moan was heard from the listeners. This part of the story was always painful.

'Our ancestors set up barriers, and men took up weapons at night to guard their families, but still the slave masters kept coming. The chief called a village meeting to discuss what to do. Back then, we had a fetish priest as well as a sorceress, Great-Grandmother. All the villagers were grief-stricken by the losses they had suffered of family and friends. "What will we do?" they cried, but the elders had no answers.

'Then our great fetish priest stood up. "I have had a vision!" he cried out. "There is a place far away from here, a safe place hidden in the jungle. A tall tree guards it. We must leave our home and go there, or we will be taken away and die as a people!"

'Our ancestors cried even more at this, but the chief said, "We must think about this. The gods have spoken through our priest. I will meet with our elders to decide what to do." Then he sent the people away and went with the priest and the obeah woman into his hut.

'That night, Great-Grandmother left her body to soar high above the land on the wings of her totem animal, the spotted eagle owl. She flew through the forest, looking for the tree. Just before the dawn time, a storm came with thunder, lightning, and pouring rain. She thought she would die. Then lightning struck a great tree in front of her. Its highest stem burst into flames like a great torch, and she saw the tree that she was searching for. She flew back to her own body and told the fetish priest what she had found.

'"I saw a great tree struck by lightning. I could see nothing . . . then the lightning struck, and the top of the tree burned like a torch. The tree is in a clearing on a hill with forest all around. There is a river to the west and a road to the east. The fire god showed me! Look for a tree with a great black spear rising above the forest on the top of a hill between a river and a road."

'The priest led our strongest men through the jungle to find our great tree'—she pointed to the Sentinel Tree above her—'and made a path for our people to follow. The chief put the plan to the people. Our ancestors debated for many days, but when another raider stole two more children, they made up their minds to move.

'The fetish priest and his men were gone for so long that our ancestors almost gave up hope, until their obeah woman saw a fire with our men gathered round beneath this tree in a dream. There was much rejoicing when they came back, and preparations were made for the journey.

'Oh, it was long and hard.' Grandmother sighed. 'I was a small child, but I had to walk most of the way, though my older sister carried me when I was too tired.

'We walked for the rising of two moons before we came to this place. After your ancestors arrived, the fetish priest and his men changed the forest into a maze. They planted trees in the path we had taken and made new paths that wound round and round, taking anyone who used them back out of our forest rather than bringing them to us.

'That is why we have been safe all this time. That is why you children must be silent when we tell you to.' Most of the children were in bed, but Grandmother looked beyond the tribe and up at Kisa, who thought she had been hidden in her tree. 'There are devils in the form of men out there who would steal you from your families, and you would never see them again.

'But a time is coming!' Her voice rose as she finished with prophecy. 'There will rise up a leader among us. Someone with great power, who will drive away the white devils so that we may return to our land by the sea!'

Others wondered who that would be. Kisa had no doubts. She was that leader. She silently vowed to drive away the white devils and lead her people home.

Chapter 3

The Slave Master's Son

Agadez was the gate to the desert. It was the city of the slave masters—men who have been funnelling captives from southern Africa through the pass and across the desert to the slave markets of the Mediterranean for at least three thousand years. They had been Muslims for about three hundred years by 1620; before that they had practiced the religions of Africa. The people of Agadez represented both northern Arab and southern Bantu bloodlines, and the prejudice existed that the whiter your skin, the better you were.

In Agadez, around 1600, a beautiful Swahili concubine, trapped in the harem of a wealthy Arab slave master, gave birth to a son. Being black-skinned and illegitimate, the baby was ignored by his father until he survived his first year. Then Master Abbad took no more interest beyond giving the baby a name.

'He will be called Sefu, because he will live by the sword.'

His mother was young, so her master's four wives and many older concubines ruled her life. Their children ruled over Sefu until he was old enough to be put to work. Those who were bullied become the bullies of the next generation. Cruelty breeds hatred as surely as kindness breeds love.

Sefu's father, Mbwana (Master) Abbad, was the son of a son of slave traders going far back in time. He was rich enough Sefu never suffered from a lack of food or material possessions. But his early life was filled with anger, hatred, and cruelty. His many half-brothers were always fighting viciously to curry their father's favour.

The firstborn ruled without question. The other legitimate sons were his companions in terror over the concubines' sons. The younger the concubine, the lower her sons were in the pecking order, and there was no doubt that the blacker the child, the less rank he could attain. Though Sefu loved his mother, he grew to hate the darkness of his skin. No mercy was given to him anywhere within the household compound.

Kisa's village was a playground in comparison. She and her peers were roughly equal in the eyes of the village, although the sons of the chiefs and his lieutenants did tend to lord it over the others. But Kisa stood up to them, and they respected her. Sefu, by contrast, was teased and tormented, beaten and driven back to his mother's skirts until he learned to fight back in anger and hatred.

One day a week, the sons of Mbwana Abbad went with him to pray at the mosque. Sefu hated it because Abbad never noticed him. Sefu had to stand at the back with only a few smaller boys behind him. He had no use for prayers and scorned those who did. The call to prayer sounded out five times a day, but whenever he could, Sefu hid instead of answering it.

When Sefu was twelve, he was put to work. Since his father was the most important slave master in Agadez, there was only one profession open to him. He became an apprentice slaver in one of the raiding parties that went south each year to capture and sell black villagers.

As soon as he joined, Sefu wanted to become the best of the slavers. He wanted to prove himself and to be able to say to that mean old man on his deathbed, 'See? I was the best! You should have chosen me!'

Sefu was apprenticed to his uncle Abdel, who had always been a raider and would never be anything else. Abdel was a cruel man who drove his nephew hard and his black raiders even harder. He was hated by all who came into contact with him, but he didn't care. His only desire was to get as many captives as he could and then get home again to spend his money on drinks and whores.

The first season, his uncle considered Sefu to be his personal servant, ordering him to do the most menial chores. Sefu hated this and longed to prove himself, so he worked hard and performed all the tasks demanded by his uncle.

Eventually Abdel allowed him to hold the horses during raids. In one, a villager ran towards Sefu, determined to capture a horse and escape. Sefu drew his knife and stabbed the man in the leg, bringing him down. Sefu jumped on his back and held him till Abdel arrived with chains. After that, Sefu was allowed to take part in the raids. Sefu was soon adept at capturing victims and chaining them together for the long march to the markets.

Twice a year, they returned to their father's quarters to give him the profits of the raids and receive their share. At first, Sefu's share was a pittance, but as he grew more skilled in his job, his father rewarded him with a fine black horse and a greater share of the profits.

When he was eighteen, an arrow pierced his uncle's armour, and Abdel died a slow, cruel death from the infected wound. No one mourned. The raiding party was passed into Sefu's hands at last. The first thing he did was give himself a second name. His raiders could no longer call him just Sefu. He was Mbwana Sefu from then on.

Zuberi, Uncle Abdel's second in command, was the first to raise the cry 'Mbwana Sefu!' The rest followed quickly, as no one wanted to be seen as hesitant in recognising their new lord. Mbwana Sefu was the son of Mbwana Abbad after all, even if a bastard. Even Abdel's most loyal lieutenants joined in loudly to show their new allegiance. They knew of too many times when the new leader had old lieutenants killed to prevent conflict within the group. It was a case of be loyal now or risk a knife in the dark.

The best part of previous visits at home had been seeing his mother. But when he returned this time, he found she had died. It was as if the world had struck back at him just as he was finally making a success of himself. She was the only person who would have rejoiced at his advancement. In his grief, the last shreds of love and compassion were burned out of his heart. There was no one left in the world who loved him or he loved in turn. There would never be another.

Still grieving, Sefu reported to his father as the commander of a raiding party. His father called him forward.

'So Abdel is dead. Good riddance. He was lazy and greedy.' Sefu's eyes narrowed at this. No one he knew was any lazier or greedier than his fat father.

'I see you have taken charge of your men. Well done. I expect better things from you than from your uncle. You are ambitious. I like that in my captains. You will be rewarded if you perform well.'

Abbad stopped, looking thoughtful. Then he motioned to a servant. 'Fetch me that bastard Badru from the women's quarters.' Abbad sat back, sipping tea while Sefu waited impatiently. Even now, he was not offered a seat or tea. He too was still a bastard in the old man's eyes.

The servant returned with a soft-faced boy of about twelve years. He was an Arab-Swahili mix like Sefu, the son of another concubine. *He's scared*, Sefu thought scornfully, even though he had been scared of his father at that age too.

'Badru! This is your older brother, Sefu. He is now the commander of your late Uncle Abdel's troops. You will serve him and learn your trade.' Abbad smiled at Sefu. 'Train him as well as Abdel trained you!' With a wave of his hand, he dismissed both of them. 'Bring back gold and guns!' he called out to Sefu's back.

Badru had to run to keep up with Sefu's long stride. When he reached the courtyard, Sefu turned on him, striking him hard across the face for no reason. 'You are mine now. Do everything I say, or there will be hell to pay.' It felt good to have someone to bully.

After that, visits to Agadez involved only time spent at the compound to report to his father, rest, and then begin preparations for the next expedition. He still hated his father, but he wanted to impress the old man, and more importantly, he wanted to become rich so he could eventually live like his father as a respected member of the Agadez community.

Sefu also used his visits to Agadez for revenge on those who had tormented him in the past. Now that he was a blooded slaver, everybody younger or smaller had best give him a wide berth. He left the dirty work to his underlings, the members of his slaving gang. In particular, his two main lieutenants Zuberi and one-eyed Kondro loved wreaking vengeance on the men who had beaten and harassed their leader when he was a boy.

Badru was now Sefu's personal servant, just as he had been to his uncle. Every menial task was performed by the boy, who was beaten if he was not quick enough. Badru quickly turned surly and unpleasant to everyone around him except Sefu, whom he hated and feared above all others.

Once Sefu took over, the raiding party quickly learned how ambitious their new leader was. He intended to get rich, and his followers could only benefit from this. Their loyalty paid off. Their Mbwana Sefu was intent on leading them to new hunting grounds, rich with potential captives. His band of raiders would follow him anywhere, especially Zuberi and Kondro.

'I am going west,' he said one night. 'The Portuguese have set up trading forts on the western shores. They pay much better for slaves. And they pay in guns and iron.' Zuberi and Kondro nodded in agreement. No one else spoke. It was not their place to argue.

The slave masters at work.

Chapter 4

The Leopard Strikes

Kisa had a happy home life. Her mother, Ama, was gentle and loving with her youngest child, and her father, Thimba, was protective and indulgent where his smallest daughter was concerned. She loved it when he carried her on his shoulders to the gardens each day. She played with the other children in the dirt while he and the other adults chipped and weeded, planted and harvested the yams and other root crops that they depended on for survival.

Kisa loved his strength and the vivid white scars on his arm and leg. Her mother told her with pride that her father was called Thimba because he had attacked a rogue leopard that had been preying on the people for months.

'He stabbed it with his knife and cut its throat as it was dragging his cousin away. It clawed him before it escaped. The woman is Aya. She lived but lost her arm.' Kisa had often wondered why Aya had only one arm. She was proud of her father for saving her.

'Grandmother saved them both. There was blood everywhere. She had to take Aya's arm off to save her. Then Grandmother sewed up the gashes on your father's arm and leg. That is where he got the scars.'

Hearing this, Kisa was sure Thimba could protect her from anything. She knew that with him near, she was safe.

The relationship between a beloved daughter and her father is very special. Kisa loved her father unconditionally, and Thimba loved her the same way. From the time she could crawl, she followed him everywhere. He loved nothing more than holding her and cuddling her, chucking her up in the air to hear her squeal, tickling her to hear her laugh, and holding her close with complete love.

For Kisa, Thimba was the first man in her life. He was perfect to her: his dark eyes, curly hair, strong muscles, chocolate skin, and his long-legged stride. Everything he did was perfect to her.

When Thimba saw the signs from Grandmother that this girl child was different, that she had noble tasks for her, he sought only to encourage her and train her in all that he knew. So Thimba took her with him everywhere from that first day when he introduced her to the tribe. He taught her all he knew even before she could climb trees. Those big black eyes watched his every move, and that small body was carried in his arms wherever he went, except when he put her in Ama's loving arms to be fed.

As soon as she could walk, she toddled after him all around the village, in the forest, and in the gardens. She watched him perform all the chores of a man of the tribe, from hunting for bush meat and fishing for the food in the streams to gardening for hours each day, tending the foods on which their lives depended. Soon, she was hoeing and weeding beside him for hours each day, building up her muscles and stamina in a timeless farm-girl way. She was never a chubby baby, but slim and spare, with long muscular limbs and a long slim neck that gave her every movement a sinuousness that was almost hypnotic.

The love that Thimba gave Kisa helped her become what she was, and she never forgot that. It was a pure love and belief in her that wrapped around her like a warm cloak and a shield against her enemies. Long after his physical presence had left her, he was with her in spirit, and the more danger she was in, the closer he was to her.

One day, Kisa, now four years old, was wandering alone beyond the edge of the village and the small clearings around it where their crops were grown. She had tired of hoeing and weeding and told her father she was going for a drink of water. But instead of going back to the village, she headed for a small stream deep in the forest that her father had shown her. Thimba liked to fish there, and he usually brought Kisa on his shoulders, but the last time they came, he made her walk ahead and find the way.

This day, she struck out confidently, following the animal tracks to a little pond created by rocks above, which narrowed it down to a waterfall that cascaded into the pool and then crept out again below through a small opening in the next set of rocks.

Her strong legs carried her swiftly by the subtle landmarks that showed the way through the endless forest. To her surprise, the trees helped her too. If she strayed even a bit from the correct pathway, the breezes in the leaves whispered, 'That way, that way.' And when her steps were true, she could feel their approval. She came out into the sunshine and knelt down to drink. While she sipped the cool, clear water, she suddenly felt eyes watching her.

She looked up to see a she-leopard crouching on the rock above her. She could have leaped on Kisa, but she did not. Instead she stared deep into Kisa's eyes and soul. Her great yellow eyes gave no hint to Kisa of what the leopard was thinking, but she felt no danger. Kisa straightened her back and stretched to her full height. Slowly she raised her right arm in a salute.

Back in the garden, Thimba had noticed that Kisa was missing. He walked over to where the village girls were gossiping around the water jars that they had carried up the hill from the river to water the gardens. 'Where is Kisa? She came for a drink.'

A chill ran through him when they answered, 'We have not seen her. She did not come here for water.' He turned and ran back through the gardens. She was nowhere to be seen. Panicking, he remembered taking her through the forest to the secret spring.

He bounded down that path as memories unbidden rose in his mind: The leopard leaping out of the jungle on his cousin and savaging her. Her screams and the animal roaring. Thimba running to her, leaping on the back of the beast and stabbing it until it turned, threw him off, raked his arm and leg with its claws, and then ran back into the jungle.

Thimba ran faster, terrified by the thought of Kisa in those savage jaws. His cousin was much bigger and only lost an arm. The leopard could kill small Kisa with one bite.

Thimba came to a halt at the spring. There before him was his worst nightmare—and yet so different. The leopard and Kisa were eye to eye across the water. Kisa was saluting it. The leopard lifted its glance to Thimba for an instant before returning her gaze to Kisa. Only an annoyed lash of the tail acknowledged his presence.

Thimba held his breath and didn't move. Then the leopard rose, stretched, and yawned. With one last glance at Kisa, it turned and padded back into the jungle. Kisa saw as she left that it was a great she-leopard.

Kisa lowered her arm but stood standing and watching for a moment, then turned to go and saw Thimba behind her. He dropped to his knees and gathered her into his arms, thanking the Great Mother for saving her.

'What's the matter, Father?'

Thimba didn't know whether to be angry or not. He begged her not to come here alone again and then carried her on his shoulder back to the village.

After lunch, the family always rested in the heat of the day, so Kisa had a chance to visit Grandmother. She burst in to the old woman's hut and saw her preparing herbs for a coming birth. 'Guess what I saw today, Grandmother!'

'The leopard.'

Kisa looked disappointed. 'How did you know?'

'Do you think I would not know when your totem animal comes to you? But tell me about her. Where were you? What did she do?'

'But you saw everything.'

Grandmother smiled. 'No, only her eyes. They came to me suddenly as I was having my tea this morning. Tell me what happened.'

'I went for a drink at the fishing hole. I didn't even look up from the water till after I drank.'

Grandmother shook her head at this. 'You were not fully aware, Kisa. You should have seen her first. Do not be so careless in the future,' she said, but secretly she was pleased at the audacity of the child to go so far alone and with no fear. *Fear will come later, with wisdom*, she thought.

'Oh, she was beautiful! Her eyes were as yellow as the sun. She was sitting on the great rock on the other side of the stream. Even her tail was still. She was just watching me. As soon as I stood up, she looked straight in my eyes. I could not move. It was . . . it was like being turned to stone.' Kisa searched for the right words.

'Then she got up and went back into the forest. I saw a cub in the shadows. I saluted her before she left.' Kisa raised her arm to show Grandmother how.

'That is good. You must always respect the spirits of the animals that choose to help you. Her courage will always be with you, Kisa. She is special to you. Tell no one about her for now. They will chide you for going alone into the forest. And I want you to be more careful in the future too! But it is a great thing for this she-leopard to honour you this way. You can call on her strength whenever you need it, my child. Now go,' she finished. 'It is hot and this old woman needs rest.'

Kisa went.

She went straight to the Sentinel Tree to tell him of her adventure. High up in the branches of her tree, she sat on a strong branch and told the tree about the leopard.

'Tell me' the leaves whispered, so she did, telling her best friend everything that had happened and all about the leopard. And then she said, 'Trees whispered to me, like you, when I go right.'

'Good . . .' the leaves whispered. 'Leopard . . . friend . . . trees . . . friends . . . listen . . . never be lost . . . we know you . . .'

'How?'

The leaves rustled, her eyes closed, and she saw something marvellous—roots. Roots of the tree spreading out, but not brown—brilliant, glowing yellow-white bands of light going off in all directions and connecting to all the trees.

'Thank you, brother tree,' Kisa remembered to say as she climbed down and went home.

Chapter 5

Events in the Outside World

Kisa's world was insular, protected by the forest and the maze, but events were occurring in the world outside that would affect her life and all those she knew. She was born in 1617 when the result of the European quest for spices, gold, colonies, and slaves was beginning to affect the native peoples of three continents: Africa, South America, and North America.

It began with spices. Europe loved pepper and other exotic spices from the Far East, as well as many other products, like silk, that they couldn't get at home. The people of the Middle East had controlled the world markets for hundreds of years, but all that began to change in the 1400s when the first European explorers found the sea route around Africa to India and China. Africa was seen primarily as an obstacle on the road to the east, but it was also known for the fabulous wealth of the fabled empires of West Africa and especially the legendary city Timbuktu, which many Europeans had heard of but none had ever seen.

Contrary to popular opinion, many Europeans thought that the earth was round. But they didn't think anyone could sail west from Europe and get anywhere. In fact, it was hard to sail west across the North Atlantic because off the coast of the British Isles and Europe, the winds and the currents travel the other direction and push everything from west to east. Anyone who tried to sail that way got blown back. The Vikings made it to Greenland and beyond because they went north and they rowed.

European ships could sail south, though. The Spanish and Portuguese found the Atlantic Islands of the Canaries and Cape Verde first. There, in the fifteenth century, they planted sugar cane in the tropical warmth and sold it at great profit to sugar-hungry Europeans. Further south, they found the lands and peoples of sub-Saharan Africa and then the first sea route to India and China, when Vasco de Gama rounded the bottom of Africa into the Indian Ocean in 1497.

It was a long way around Africa, so it was necessary to create places where ships could safely stop. Africa was not as dark as popular history made out, but it was still dangerous for outsiders. In fact, the tropical West African coast become known as the White Man's Grave. But it was also a place to trade for gold, ivory, and valuable timbers.

For centuries, salt and other goods moved south from the Mediterranean by camels across the desert to Timbuktu or Agadez, the two great cities that were the gates to the desert, and then on south across the entire African continent on trade routes by land and by river that are still being used to this day. Timbuktu was important because it was built on the banks of the great Niger River. It was said that Timbuktu was where the ships of the desert met the ships of the river, and so the goods from the north could move easily for thousands of miles across all sub-Saharan Africa.

In the great rainforests of Central Africa, the jungle was so thick that all long-distance traffic had to go by river. The Niger was one of the most important rivers because it was so long that it could bring the riches of the north to many different forest tribes.

The main traders in the north were the Arabs and the Tuaregs. To the south, the main traders were Swahili-speaking Bantu people. These people had been trading for thousands of years, including slaving. To this day, Swahili is the universal language of trade in sub-Saharan Africa. It is the native language of only two million people, but twenty million people can speak it as a kind of universal second language in Africa, useful in business and trade.

Timbuktu was a legendary city in Europe, known to be a city of gold but unattainable. No one crossed the desert unless the Tuareg and Arab traders allowed it. Like the Silk Road in the east, they wanted to keep the routes hidden. European explorers didn't reach Timbuktu until the 1800s, long after the sea lanes were conquered and the coast covered in trading forts, slave castles, and white colonizers.

Slavery was common throughout Africa and Asia, including Europe, for thousands of years. Despite slavery, Africa was not any more uncivilized than the peoples of other continents. Art, metalworking, weaving, and other crafts flourished. Some of the most so-called primitive tribes practiced sophisticated forms of democracy. There was warfare and witchcraft for sure, but there was also great environmental and botanical knowledge and sophisticated societies that could be as enlightened as any Greek city state.

Then came the Europeans. The first wooden trading fort south of the Sahara was built by the Portuguese only a few miles from the original village of Kisa's people, on the coast of what is now Ghana at a place called Axim. They started it in 1472, and by 1482, when it was visited by the explorer Christopher Columbus, they were actively trading for cocoa, ivory, timbers, and other local products with the various tribes of the region.

It was no coincidence that ten years later, Columbus took his three little ships south down the coast of Africa and turned west only when he was in the South Atlantic. There is evidence in the forgotten libraries of Timbuktu that Africans had known about the land across the sea for thousands of years. The currents and winds in the South Atlantic flowed predominantly to the west. It was never easy to cross the ocean, but not impossible. And if Columbus had talked to the fishermen, they could have told him it was possible to cross the ocean to a different land. He decided that land must be India and so spent the next ten years touring the courts of the crowned heads of Europe. Finally, Queen Isabella of Spain gave him the *Pinta*, the *Niña*, and the *Santa Maria*, and the rest is history.

On his second voyage, Columbus took sugar cane with him and planted it on the Caribbean Island of Hispaniola (modern Haiti). Columbus had seen the wealthy sugar cane plantations on the Canary Islands, which were already being worked by black slaves taken from the Congo region of southern Africa.

The sugar industry was pioneered throughout the Caribbean Islands and the coastal regions of South America by the Spanish and Portuguese in the 1500s. At first, they used the local peoples as slaves in their plantations and in their mines, but the natives died of the strange diseases and proved unsuitable for the back-breaking work regime demanded by their new masters. Africans were the answer, and so the Atlantic slave trade became the essential third pillar of what became known as the Great Atlantic Trading Triangle.

Columbus may have thought he had found India, but what he immediately recognized was that these lands were rich, not only in gold but in land for growing crops and people to be used as slaves. Columbus was a slaver. He captured some of the first people he met and took them back as slaves. And he sold his discoveries, not just on the promise of gold but on the land as a place where Europeans could grow crops and become rich.

Sugar was vital from the beginning. Those who could not go adventuring around the New World looking for gold or the fountain of youth quickly turned to farming. Back home in Europe, good farmland was hard to acquire. The exodus across the sea to take advantage of all that new farmland was on as early as the 1500s, and by the early seventeenth century, the growing number of European trading forts along the coast of Africa were demanding slaves as well as timber and ivory for locals to exchange for European products.

By the 1620s, when Kisa was growing up in the seclusion of her village in the maze, the effects of the Atlantic slave trade on African life were becoming significant. The Arab-Swahili slave traders had been taking people for centuries but in small numbers. There was a limit to how many slaves could be sold. But not when the New World turned to sugar.

Sugar could not be grown in any quantity in Europe, but it thrived on the coast of Brazil, the islands of the Caribbean, and later in the southern states of the United States. The market for sugar was seemingly insatiable during an era when kings like Henry the Eighth liked to eat off plates made of sugar and then consume the plates.

That love of sugar led to the insatiable need for forced labour on the new plantations, which were totally dependent on human labour to succeed. Native Americans wouldn't work, but Africans did. They were immune to many of the diseases that plagued Native Americans, and they were hard workers. This work was beyond hard, but on average, they could survive five years of it, which made them very economical.

The Atlantic Trade Triangle went like this. Sugar and any other goods like gold and silver were taken across the North Atlantic on the easterly currents to Europe. They were sold for European goods, and then the ships sailed south to Africa. There, they exchanged those goods for slaves, which were then shipped west across the South Atlantic. And round and round it went for over three hundred years.

For the Europeans, it was great business; for Africans, it was a continent-wide cultural disaster that led ultimately to the colonization and subjugation of thousands of unique cultures. It is true that there were cannibals among them and warfare was common, but there was also art and music and culture, stories and songs and languages, which were all but wiped out in the three hundred years of the slave trade and the four hundred years of colonization by Europeans.

By the fifteenth century, the African continent was one of great cultural diversity with over a thousand separate languages or dialects. There were kingdoms and empires, such as Mali and Ethiopia, but in many parts of the continent, no major centralised states existed, and many people lived in societies where there were no great divisions of wealth and power. In such societies, there were systems of government by councils of elders that were possibly the world's first democracies.

Throughout North Africa, Islam had already begun to play a significant role by the 1500s. Further south, there was a diversity of religious and philosophical beliefs. In many areas, these beliefs remained traditional and stressed the importance of communing with the spirits of the ancestors and nature. These African societies were not just primitive savages but were following their own patterns of development before the disaster of European intervention.

The Arab-Swahili trading routes were well established in the 1600s, and they traded everything, including humans for slaves. It was a logical extension to sell to the Europeans when they began building trading forts up and down the Atlantic coast of Africa. Those forts were fought over by different European powers over time, but the end result was this: over a hundred such forts were built and used to trade slaves.

The pressure on the peoples of Africa became intense. Africa's entire population in the 1600s was probably around twenty-five million, divided into about a thousand different tribal/cultural/language groups. Over the three hundred years of the Atlantic slave trade, about that many people in total, some twenty-five million people, were captured and sold or died along the trails of tears across Africa. Fully half died before being shipped away—the rest left their homeland through gates of no return, died or survived the Middle Passage as the sea voyage was known, and then lived short brutal lives in plantations or in mines.

Some said that the peoples of Africa were like sheep or cattle, being docile to capture and domesticated and happy to serve. This was a lie to cover up the horror of what they were doing. Many peaceful tribes were wiped out in this holocaust, but some people fought back, like the people of the village in the maze, including a child destined to become the mother of her nation.

Chapter 6

Afia's Journey

Sefu was angry, always angry. Only the object of his anger changed. He was sitting on his big black horse at the head of a line of raiders who were struggling to keep up, but he didn't care. They were his slaves, though he had to pay them for their labours. They were Nyamweri, people of the moon, from a village far to the east, and they had been raiders for the Arab/ Swahili slavers since the time before time was counted.

This day, Sefu was angry because so many of the western villages were empty. Previous raiders had already captured many people and burned the villages.

'No one here,' he muttered, kicking his horse with vicious spurs through the remains of yet another empty village.

I will find them. We will just keep looking. But that thought made him angrier.

He was only twenty-five, but he was already a hardened raider. He was still handsome, but his face was scarred and his eyes hard. He was cruel and wasted no feelings for his many victims. He carried a long whip set with leather knots meant to rip through the skins of captives and the raiders he commanded alike.

He had been raiding to the west and selling to the Portuguese for months. At first, business was good, because the western villages had previously suffered little from the Arab slave trade, being too many days' march away from the markets. The slavers did not like to waste money on food or water for their victims, so if the distances to cover were too great, too many of the captives died to make it profitable. But now these villages were only a short march from the west coast where the new Portuguese owners paid in guns for captives.

Sefu spat at the thought of the Portuguese. He had been to their great slave fort several times. They paid well, so he would go back, but he didn't like them. He considered them weak and effeminate, with their brocade jackets and white ruffles. Only their guns gave them the advantage. They were not real men. He thought of the commander of the fort, a man who could barely lift a sword because of all his white man's illnesses, from gout to syphilis. He had access to the entire female slave population of the castle, and he probably only took one a week to his bed.

Sefu felt himself rousing at the thought of all those female bodies waiting in the women's quarters for someone to master them. *I would have ploughed through them in a week.*

Sefu kept moving towards the coast, and a week later, he found what he was looking for. The village was poor. Most of those in it were too old or too young to bring good prices, but Sefu didn't care. 'Take them all!' he ordered.

First to go forward was Badru, who was now allowed to carry a knife and help capture villagers. He was eager to prove himself and rise in Sefu's estimation. He ran towards the best-looking specimen in this pathetic village—a young man who looked to be worth more than the rest.

Badru already knew how to be cruel, but he was not yet a good fighter. His intended victim suddenly lifted a machete and sliced down with it, taking off half of Badru's ear and cheek and only narrowly missing his eye. Badru screamed and fell to his knees. The villager lifted his machete to kill Badru, but Sefu rode up and took the man's head off with one sweep of his sword. As the rest of the raiding party ran around him, gathering up everyone in the village, Sefu leaped down and stood over his weeping half-brother.

'You useless piece of horse dung! You should have stayed in the harem with the women! I should have let him kill you! He was worth far more to me than you are!'

Sefu kicked him and stormed off to supervise the rounding up of the last of the weeping villagers. Badru pressed a dirty cloth to his face to stop the bleeding. His ear lay on the ground, and the pain was unbearable, but no one stopped to help him.

Sefu's raiders swarmed through the half-ruined huts and grabbed everyone who was left or killed those too young or too old to sell. Some begged for mercy, but none was given. Only two escaped.

Twelve-year-old Afia had gone to the waterhole with her jar on her head and her younger brother, Kojo, running beside her. He played while she filled her jar, and she sang him a funny song about the greedy trickster Kwaku and how he cheated Brother Death by climbing his web all the way to heaven. Suddenly, screams rang out from the village. The children froze, then Afia grabbed Kojo's hand and ran into the jungle.

When night fell, Kojo wanted to go home, but Afia held him back. She pulled leaves over them and curled around him to keep them warm. They huddled in each other's arms till the dawn time and then slowly crept home. It was gone. All that was left were smoking ruins. The children crouched, stunned, afraid to go closer. Finally, when Afia was sure the raiders were gone, they ventured into the wreckage.

They found the old nannas dead, but their mother and the other women and children were gone. So were the few men of the village, even the old chief. Afia sat down near her home fireplace and cried. Kojo patted her and asked for his mother.

'She's gone! They're all gone!' Afia wailed, and Kojo fell silent. He did not speak again for a long time.

At last, Afia rose with a sigh and searched among the ruins for things she could use to keep them alive. She selected a small basket from the debris and gathered some yams and other unspoiled foods. Then she searched through the ruins of household fires until she found glowing embers buried beneath the surface of one. Carefully she gathered some in a bed of grasses placed in a small pot with a lid for this purpose, tied it shut with a piece of twine, and put it in her carry basket.

She found a broken-handled knife and an unbroken water jar. She found two lengths of cloth and draped one over her shoulder and the other over Kojo's for warmth in the nights.

Kojo picked up only one item, a small drum. He stood holding it tightly while watching his sister gather supplies. When she had finished, Afia put the water jar on her head, and with her basket in one hand and Kojo by the other, she led him away from their old life forever.

Sefu finished his raids on the remaining small villages along the coast. He arrived at the fort the Portuguese called Elmina (the mine). He took the villagers inside and sold them for enough seashells to buy guns for his raiders and whores for himself. There was enough for the trip home and to pay his father, but it was not as much as he had hoped.

Badru visited a local healer and had his wounds treated, but they were already infected. The old woman put powders on them and chanted prayers to the gods, but nothing would bring back his ear, and the scar on his face was going to be ugly. He cursed his brother but returned to the raider's camp because he had no other option, especially now. Who else would have him with such a wound? His dream of someday leading his own raiding party shattered.

Sefu, meanwhile, was talking to other slavers and soldiers in the fort. 'The prices here are better than to the east, but the villages are empty.'

They told him that the best villages for raiding were to the north on the plains. 'But there are still some good ones here. It is just that they are hidden. People have moved from the coast deeper into the jungles. You will have to be a better hunter if you want to find them.'

Sefu intended to do just that.

Once she was a safe distance from the village, Afia sat down to think. She had heard tales of a hidden village where people were safe from the slavers. All she knew was that it was a long way to the north through the jungle. She sighed at the thought but was determined to survive. So she stood up, faced north, and began walking.

They walked all day, and when night came, Afia gathered some tinder and kindling and then opened her little pot with trepidation. She was rewarded with the glow of the embers, still alive in their bed. She put them in the middle of her tinder and blew gently till she had a small fire. Quickly she heated some water in her cook pot with the yams she had collected that morning.

She decided to cook them all at once so they would have several days of food rather than risking a fire every night. She gave Kojo a small dinner of yam but ate only a mouthful herself. Both children were hungry after the long day's march, but Afia knew to hoard what she had. Who knew what food they would find on this journey?

During the next day's walk, she looked for food as she went, and she was right. In this uncultivated part of the forest, there were only a few mushrooms and herbs to be collected, but she added them to her basket. That night, she did not feel safe, so she did not build a fire, and they ate from their small stock of cold food and then huddled together in their blankets for the night.

She saw no signs of people or gardens, so Afia gathered herbs and roots and even insects and grubs as they walked. Each day, she filled her basket with whatever she could find to keep hunger at bay, but it was never enough. Monkeys and birds taunted her, but she had no way to hunt them. She used the broken-handled knife to sharpen a small wooden spear for Kojo, and between them, they sometimes caught frogs and lizards to add to the pot.

Every night, she checked her precious embers, collected anew each time she had a fire and protected as her most precious possession. If it was safe, she cooked whatever they had gathered—turning herbs and mushrooms, roots, shoots and grubs, or whatever frogs or lizards they could catch into a soup and always saving some for the next day or two. After the meal, she put the fire out for fear of it being seen by unfriendly eyes. Instead, at night, the two children huddled together with one blanket under them and one over them for warmth. Afia passed the time by singing to Kojo and telling him stories, but he never spoke.

As the moon was waning into blackness, they came to a road. It was running roughly to the north, so Afia decided to take the chance and use it to cover more distance. During the days, they hid. They walked at dusk time when the moon was rising and in the early dawn time. Sleeping in the day was more comfortable because it was warmer, but travelling at night meant it was harder to find food, and she could not risk lighting a fire to cook it.

When the road turned east, Afia headed back into the jungle. One day, she saw a baby monkey whose leg was injured.

'We catch 'im,' she whispered to Kojo. She touched her chest and said, 'Pretend eat—keep 'im looking here.' She touched Kojo's chest. 'Climb tree—catch 'im!' Kojo nodded and began climbing, while Afia got out food and pretended to eat, which kept the hungry baby's attention on her.

Kojo managed to catch him by the tail, but he turned and bit the boy. Kojo dropped the monkey, but Afia was ready with her stick. She pushed away the sadness she felt at killing a baby, and that night they feasted.

'Proper bush meat,' she told Kojo, hoping he would respond. He just kept eating. The monkey stew was delicious.

Another moon rose and fell. Afia and Kojo grew thinner, but Afia kept pushing them north, deeper into the jungle. The paths now seemed to lead in circles, and Afia despaired at finding anything in the tangled maze of brambles and thorny trees. At last, she sat beneath a forest giant and prayed to the Earth Mother. 'Only you can save us now, Mother. Show the way!' She poured a small offering of water on the earth. It was all she had.

After that, a trail north opened up for her. When she came to a dead end, she sent Kojo to crawl through the brambles, and each time he found a new path for them. They found springs of water in unlikely places and tiny patches of yams when they were most hungry. Afia pushed on, believing that the Great Mother was helping her.

'I save you,' she whispered to Kojo at night. 'We find the hidden village. Our mother taking us there.' If it comforted Kojo, she could not tell, for he did not answer her.

One bright, sunny day, Kisa was playing on the edge of the gardens when she saw them. She moved into the forest and approached the two children who were standing hand in hand, staring at her.

'Akwaaba,' she called out to them in welcome and walked up to the boy. She touched her hand to her heart and said, 'Kisa.' Then she reached out and touched Kojo on his heart.

'Kojo,' Afia heard him say, and she burst into tears.

Chapter 7

Kojo's Drum

Kisa took both children by their hands and led them into the garden. Thimba and the others dropped their tools and surrounded them. Afia found their language a bit hard to follow, but she could see by their smiles that they were welcome.

'We come there.' She pointed south. 'Village gone. We alone.'

'Akwaaba, akwaaba,' the villagers said, and the universal word for welcome among the Akan peoples reassured her. They gave the two children a drink of water and then took them back to the village. Kisa proudly led the way.

Grandmother gave them into the care of an old childless couple, Esi and Adisa. Esi was a loving woman who lost her babies before birth and longed for children even more after she passed the age of fertility. She had often prayed to the gods to help her—Afia and Kojo answered those prayers. She doted on them, and the children thrived in spite of the terrible loss they had suffered.

Adisa had longed to be a father since the day he married Esi many long years before. He too had suffered when their children were delivered stillborn. He blamed himself for some unknown sin against the gods. He was an intelligent if unlettered man who loved teaching everyone else's children with endless stories as he worked at his craft. Adisa was a master weaver and could create mats and blankets of exceptional beauty.

He felt an overwhelming love for the two skinny, bedraggled orphans from the moment Kisa led them out of the forest. He could not believe it when Grandmother said, 'Let Esi and Adisa be their mother and father. They need good, loving parents to heal them.'

Afia blossomed first. She was greatly admired for saving her brother's life. Her story was welcome at the campfires as many times as she wished to tell it. Kojo followed her wherever she went, clutching his little drum and still silent

Only the sight of Kisa brought a smile to his solemn face. She was drawn to him and sought him out often. They didn't need to speak. She sat quietly next to him while Afia talked to the other women and helped with chores.

Sometimes Kisa pulled out a few pebbles and played with them like marbles. After silently watching for a few days, Kojo picked one up and tossed it into her circle. They smiled at one another. Kisa picked up the stone and gave it to Kojo to keep.

One night, not long after they arrived, a soft drum began to beat. The master drummer was calling the people to gather together in celebration of life. Afia was excited and arrived early with her little brother, who was holding her hand and his drum. Afia chose a good vantage point near the fire, sitting on a log where she could see everything and talk to everyone. Kojo, still clutching his drum, fell asleep behind her in the shadows.

The evening was long, and the drumming went on for hours. First, the master drummer summoned his drummers, and they joined him. All through the evening, they played to his guidance, passed to them through his subtle changes in sound and rhythm. The drumming rolled through complex sections with multiple rhythms—some fast, some slow, some loud, and some soft. Each performance was unique, never to be repeated in exactly the same sequence, but there were patterns and meanings in them, and the master drummer knew them all.

All the while the people danced, feet and hands and bodies in rhythm with the drummers. It was hypnotic, and all the day's frets and fears were washed away with the dancing. Then, after the drumming ceased, the people turned to food, drink, and talk.

The master drummer walked over to Afia and greeted her, 'Akwaaba', and touched his chest, saying, 'Addy.'

'Akwaaba,' she answered, touching her breast. 'Afia.' She pointed to her brother. 'Kojo.'

Addy looked at the sleeping boy clutching his little drum. 'Play drum?'

Afia shook her head sadly. 'Him sad. No talk, no play.'

Addy knelt beside the sleeping boy and touched the drum softly. 'Someday,' he whispered.

A few days later, Addy was getting a drink from the water girls and saw Afia with Kojo. He walked over, smiled at the boy, and said, 'Good drum. It is kidi. It plays a different beat from the main drums. I will show you how to play it.'

Kojo looked up and, to Afia's amazement, handed the drum to Addy. Addy tapped out a rhythm then handed it back. Wordlessly, Kojo took the drum and repeated the rhythm perfectly.

'Come play with me, Kojo,' Addy said and turned back to his hut. Kojo followed. Afia watched them go with a smile. The healing had begun.

Within a few weeks, Kojo and Afia were accepted by all as members of the tribe. Afia assumed the role of a good daughter who helped her new mother with the chores of cooking, cleaning, and hauling water. Kojo helped his new father with gardening chores, repair of the hut, and weaving—a man's task in this village.

Whenever he could, Kojo escaped to find the master drummer, and over the next few years, Addy taught him all he knew. Kojo was smart and a born musician. He learned the different patterns and rhythms the first time he was shown each one. He loved the drum because it did his talking for him. The rhythms put him into a trance-like state where all the sorrows of his life fell away and there was nothing but the music. At gatherings, he was silent except when he was drumming, and all his emotions, pent-up since the day he lost his family, were expressed in the music.

He was accepted by the other drummers and was soon playing his kidi drum at village gatherings. It was a hard part to play because the kidi does not follow the main rhythm but goes off on its own counter beat. But Kojo seldom made a mistake and never more than once.

While Kojo was learning to drum, Kisa was growing up, but she was still a wild child with none of the concentration for a single task that Kojo was showing. She wanted to climb trees or go hunting, and she loved to play rough-and-tumble games. She had no use for dolls or babies and preferred gardening and carrying water to the homelier chores of cooking and cleaning.

Hide-and-seek was her favourite game. She loved the strange, gut-wrenching fear and excitement she got when she was being chased. She loved to win the game by making it safely back to the Sentinel Tree at the centre of the village, which was designated home safe. Her tree always shivered with excitement when she touched his skin in one of these games.

Early in life, the children were taught what to do if the slavers came. If the alarm was sounded, the children were to scatter into the forest and hide. When Kojo came out of his shell, he became Kisa's chief competitor in this game. He was several years older and was as good at hiding as and better at dodging chasers than Kisa. His cheeky grin when he won home first was both attractive and annoying to her.

Kojo knew by this time that he loved Kisa. Whenever he could, he played with her so he could hear her laugh and look into her sparkling eyes. By the time he was ten and Kisa was seven, a year after he arrived, he knew that he would marry her. He was competitive and made sure that he won all his fights with the other boys so that she could see what a strong man he was becoming.

One day, when he could see that the boy was maturing into a man, Chief Abrafo took Kojo aside and explained to him that his village had been destroyed by slavers. 'You must become a warrior and avenge your people when you grow up.'

Kojo nodded. 'I want to do that. Will you teach me?'

'Of course. Adisa is a good weaver, but he is no warrior. Come to me each day. Follow me, and I will teach you to hunt, to kill game, and to use weapons. One day, I believe you will be a great warrior.' Chief Abrafo sighed.

'We need warriors in these times. The slavers will come here someday. They are relentless. No matter how hard we try and hide, they will find us again. We must be ready.'

Kojo drew himself up tall. 'I can do that. I will be ready, my chief.'

Chief Abrafo smiled at the strong young lad. 'I believe you, boy. You will be a great help to us.'

Kojo and Afia's life settled back into the familiar patterns of village life. Kojo learned how to drum—he loved this more than anything and practiced whenever he could. He also learned to weave with Adisa and hunt with Chief Abrafo and the other men. In his free time, he played chase games with Kisa and the other children or helped in the gardens.

Afia helped Esi with the cooking and cleaning, carried water, and played with the village babies. In her free time, she liked to giggle and gossip with her new sisters and aunties and eye the young men. The girls braided and played with each other's hair, sang songs, and told stories in the easy friendship of young girls everywhere. They also discussed all the fears and difficulties of their lives—the slavers, the food supply, the girl issues like menstruation and pregnancy—and supported each other at many levels, as sisters do.

Both orphans found happiness in their new lives, and the memories of their old lives slipped away into the dim recesses of distant memory. The years passed, and the children grew into adolescence.

Chapter 8

The Coming of the Twins

A year after Afia and Kojo came to the village, the twins came into Kisa's life. Much as she loved the rest of her family, she loved the twins more, for they were as close to her as if she had borne them herself.

Kisa sensed the twins from the moment of their creation. That night, as she lay sleeping, oblivious to the sounds of her parents making love across the room, she had a dream. In that dream, she saw a beautiful young woman and her twin, a handsome young man. They were holding hands, smiling at her, and surrounded by pulsating beams of light radiating out from them. She knew they were her sister and brother. She smiled and ran towards them, and the dream ended in a glorious sense of oneness with these two new beings in her life.

The next morning, Kisa woke with the rooster's crow long before dawn because of the full moon. She bounced off her mat and went over to her parents, who still tolerated her jumping on them and then crawling in-between them for as long as they could lie there before the day's work began.

This morning, she bounced and screamed in her still high-pitched baby girl voice, 'Ama! Papa! I saw them! Our new babies!' Nothing they could say silenced her. Finally, Ama managed to settle Kisa under the covers. 'What are you talking about?' she asked her excited youngest child.

'There are babies in you, Ama! Father put them in you last night!' was the astonishing answer. Both parents stopped breathing for a time.

'Nonsense, Kisa, it was a dream.'

'Yes, Ama, a dream! I saw them! I held them! I feel them now . . .' And with that, Kisa snuggled down between her mother's ample breasts and into her stomach, wrapping her arms around and holding so tightly that it took Ama ages to pry her loose so she could get up and fetch water.

Kisa ran to Grandmother. 'Nana, Nana!' she called out as she pushed aside the mat covering the old obeah woman's doorway. 'There are babies coming!'

'Hush, child. Do not speak of them yet. The spirits are listening, and not all of them are good. Protect them by not speaking of them. Come with me today. It is time you learned the names of the medicine plants in the forest. Fetch me my basket.'

Kisa was amazed. She had been following Grandmother and the other women when they gathered plants for food and medicine since she could walk. As soon as she could talk, she was asking questions, but the women only taught her about the foods. The other plants were taboo to her. And now Grandmother was going to take her with her to find medicines! Silently she fetched two baskets and cloths to cover them and followed the obeah woman into the jungle.

When her mother was three months along in the pregnancy, Kisa felt the babies move. By that time, Ama knew she was pregnant, although she prayed that Kisa was wrong about there being two of them. She felt tired, not strong enough for this pregnancy, much less a double dose of babies to care for. Ama kept the secret of her pregnancy from all but Grandmother and her husband in case she miscarried. She was already a grandmother herself and her tight, curly hair was far more white than black.

She told Kisa to keep quiet about it too. Kisa understood. After Grandmother's talk, she knew that there were evil spirits who could harm newborn babies, and she intended to protect the twins. She didn't even tell Kojo, who was by now her best friend.

As the pregnancy advanced to the point where it was obvious to all, Grandmother became more and more concerned about Ama. She was thin, and her teeth were beginning to fall out as her body used the calcium to make the babies' bones.

Grandmother made sure to spend time with Ama every day. She gave her herbs, helped with her chores, and barked orders at Kisa, whose own workload increased too. Kisa didn't mind. She was tired of childish games, except hide, and wanted to help her mother and the twins, as she already felt responsible for them.

She could see her mother's weakness but had no fear for the twins. They were coming one way or the other. She swallowed the fear she felt for her Ama and helped her wherever she could, rubbing her back and her feet as the pregnancy progressed.

Kisa believed completely in Grandmother's ability to help Ama. She knew the old medicine woman had seen hundreds of births and would know what to do whatever happened.

Ama was not surprised the day Grandmother informed her that there were two babies growing in her body. She resigned herself to the knowledge of the coming double birth.

'I think it will be early,' Grandmother muttered one day after examining Ama. Kisa started to cheer, but Grandmother hushed her. 'Too early. We must try to keep them in as long as she can bear it, but they cannot go for the full time. It will be too much for her.'

When they came, it was the worst situation the old obeah woman could imagine. The babies were almost too early to survive, and they were lying the wrong way to come out easily when Ama's water broke and she went into labour.

What should have been easy after ten previous pregnancies was not. Ama could not push the first baby out, which was jammed sideways against her pelvis. After hours and hours, she had used all her energy, and there was nothing left for the battle. She sagged back into the birth chair and gave up.

Grandmother knew what must happen next. She did not call it a caesarean section, having never heard of Caesar, but she knew how to do it, as previous obeah women had been doing it for millennia.

Quietly she had Kisa and her two midwife assistants lift Ama off the chair and on to mats on the floor of her hut.

'Fetch me more clean cloths,' she said to one woman, and to Kisa, she said, 'Fetch me the mixture in the jar with the star and sun on it.' Kisa got it, knowing that it held sticky black goo that made a person sleep soundly regardless of the pain.

Grandmother used a small wooden spoon to give Ama the painkiller. As Ama drifted off to sleep, she slipped a stick into her mouth for her to bite on against whatever pain she still felt. Then Grandmother cleaned the lower abdomen area and her sharpest knife with hot water. Suddenly, with a motion as swift as a serpent, she cut a hand-sized slice in Ama's lower belly. Ama screamed as Kisa held her hand tight, and Grandmother reached in and pulled the first twin. *The boy*, registered Kisa's mind as the obeah's assistant grabbed the babe in clean cloth, and Grandmother went back in for the second babe.

A lot of blood was flowing by this time, but the obeah's second assistant was sopping it up as fast as she could. With some manoeuvring, Grandmother's sure hand guided the head of the second child out of the womb. The girl, Kisa saw.

Everything was happening too fast for it all to register in Kisa's mind. Her mother passed out, but the other three women were all action. As quickly as she could, Grandmother removed the placentas from the womb so she could use the thread and needles she had at the ready to sew up the cut she had made.

While she sewed up Ama, the other two women tended to the babes, first clearing their mouths and helping them take their first breaths, then wiping them clean with warm, wet rags and wrapping them in clean blankets. They used vine strings to cut off the blood in the two umbilical cords, but it was up to the obeah to cut the cords.

Grandmother pressed clean rags against Ama's newly stitched belly to sop up the last of the blood. She covered her and gave her an herbal potion to help her heal. Then she turned to the babies. She made sure the cords were properly tied, chanted the appropriate blessings and incantations to protect them, then cut them free from the placentas.

The two assistants moved quickly to clean everything up while the obeah inspected the screaming twins and then firmly attached them to Ama's nipples.

'Fetch me a cup of water,' Grandmother said at last as she sat back with a sigh. The birth was over. The twins had arrived.

When they were three months old and sure to survive, Kisa's father took them out for all to see. He held them up to the sky and named them. The boy was to be called Kwame after the day of the week on which he was born. The little girl was named Shani, which meant *marvellous*.

The months after the birth were the busiest Kisa had ever known. Her older sisters helped too, but other than nursing, Ama could do nothing. So Kisa fetched and carried and looked after the twins. She changed them, bathed them, and played with them. In every free moment, when they were sleeping with their mother, she was helping Obeah.

Kisa knew somehow that she was the obeah's apprentice. It was as if the birthing was a test and Kisa had passed. Wherever Grandmother went, Kisa was with her if her baby duties allowed. And as the twins grew older and more independent, Kisa spent more and more time following the village obeah and learning her craft.

Kisa learned the uses of the plants, how to prepare them, and what made them dangerous. She helped Grandmother preserve them and store them in specially marked jars that lined the edges of her hut.

She went with the obeah to treat the sick and deliver the babies. She helped clean up after and listened with care to all the chants and blessings that Grandmother muttered as well as the medicines that she used. Spiritual and physical, it was all intertwined, and the words were as important as the medicine.

She learned how to make potions and how to chant the songs that went with them and gave them power in the minds of those who asked for them.

PART 2

1631-1641

Chapter 9

Discovered!

Sefu was angry again. His raiders had been hacking their way through the underbrush and brambles for days, and still there was nothing to be found for their troubles. And what troubles they had been for the sweaty bare backs of the raiding party. Sefu's lieutenants, Kondo and Zuberi, used their leather whips whenever the workers slacked off in the unrelenting tropical heat. Badru followed, his face still raw and oozing pus.

They cursed their way forward as brambles scratched them and whips drove them on. Then at last they found a sign. A cloth doll had been dropped on a footprint in the track. There was a village ahead!

Kisa, now seven, was high up the Sentinel Tree when she heard the tree whisper to her, 'Danger!' She looked out and saw something strange. Far off in the distance was a beast with two heads. One was an animal head and the other was a man whose eyes were staring straight at her. When Sefu saw the small girl child in a tree, he knew he had found his prey.

For a second, Kisa was mesmerised by the evil she saw in those dark eyes. Then she tore her eyes away and called down to Kojo, who was below her on a stronger branch that could hold his weight. She pointed, and when he saw the stranger on the horse, he let out a warning cry to the villagers below.

'Come down now, Kisa!' he ordered as the adults sprang into action. 'They are enemies! We must hide!' Both children descended to the ground and took off towards the forest.

The next sound was a gunshot, the first Kisa had ever heard. The men grabbed whatever tools or weapons were at hand and ran towards the sound, while the women rounded up the children and headed out of the village in all directions.

Kisa needed no urging. She ran as fast as her little legs could pump out the steps, dodging between huts and trees, crouching low so as not to be seen. She dived down a gully into the brambles and crouched there, covering herself in sticks and leaves and trying to control her ragged breathing. Kojo was right behind her and crouched with her, putting his arms around her to protect her.

High above her, she saw the black horse carrying a swarthy but not-quite black man with a scarred face. He had a whip in his hand and was barking out orders, it seemed, to other men who were racing by him to look for villagers. The raiders were as black as she, but different. They wore strange clothes and spoke a different tongue, though some of the words sounded vaguely like her own.

She put her head down and willed herself invisible. She felt safe in Kojo's strong arms. The raiders passed; there were cries in the distance. Eventually there was silence, but still the two children stayed in their hideout. Around her, the trees whispered to her, 'They will not see you. We will protect you.'

Then they heard again the dreaded sound of the raiders, who were barking commands amidst the wails of the villagers who had been captured. Kisa looked up to see some of her tribe bound together and surrounded by their captors as they stumbled by on the ridge above her. The bearded man on the horse brought up the rear. He looked ugly in his anger. Behind him was a man even uglier, missing an ear and with a terrible wound that turned his face into a frightening mask of evil and hatred.

Kisa watched as they passed. A slight sigh of relief escaped her lips when she saw that her parents and Grandmother were not among the captives, but Kojo was distraught to see his gentle stepfather, Adisa, with a chain on his neck. Kojo trembled at the sight, but he knew not to call out.

Then they were gone, and the silence returned, but Kisa and Kojo did not move. Kisa felt as if she had been turned to stone. It was only when evening deepened and the earth cooled that they finally moved slowly out of the brambles and up the hill.

They crept back to the village and slowly moved into the circle of huts. Kojo saw Kisa home and went off to find Afia and Esi, who were grieving the loss of Adisa.

Ama was lying in bed with the twins and surrounded by her older children. When Ama saw Kisa, she sobbed and grabbed the child, holding her close. Her brothers and sisters joined them and all clung to one another, sobbing. Father stood by protectively, relieved that Kisa and the older children had found safety in the forest.

When the raid began, Thimba went straight to his hut, where Ama and the twins were huddled, for she was too weak to carry them to the safety of the forest. Thimba saw that Kisa was not there, but he swallowed his fears for her and turned to face the raiders to protect his wife and new babies. In his hands were only his knife and a hoe, but the look on his face was enough to turn Sefu's raiders aside to find easier prey. Thimba could not save the village, but he was ready to die to protect Ama and their children. He was Kisa's rock, always there for his family.

Mother kept her close all that night, but in the morning, as soon as Kisa could, she made her way to Grandmother's hut to see how she had fared.

'Grandmother!' Kisa cried out as she hugged the old woman. 'I was so scared for you! You cannot run fast like me! I thought they took you!'

At that, Grandmother laughed. 'What do they want with an ugly old woman? They were looking for beautiful women and strong young men. I stayed in my hut and put curses on their heads when they looked in, so they kept moving.'

'Where do they come from?' Kisa wanted to know everything. She was rewarded with a story while Grandmother fixed them a hot drink.

'That is a mystery,' she began. 'The black ones have always come for more lives than we can count back. We call them the people of the moon because they come from where the moon rises, and they used to go back that way when they got what they wanted. Mostly they took young women and a few strong men. And although most never returned, some did.'

Grandmother sat silent for a moment, thinking. 'Do you remember the story of an old woman who returned from the east? She told me that she was taken all the way to the eastern ocean to a big city called Zanzibar from which many people sailed, most never to be seen again.'

'Once, her master took her on a trip across the sea. They journeyed to the country of his birth, called Ind. It was a strange land where the people and the trees were very different, and some rode elephants!'

Kisa snorted at this and looked at Grandmother with wide-eyed disbelief. She had seen forest elephants, and they were strong wild animals that no one here ever rode.

'I know it is hard to believe, but you will see stranger things when you grow up, Kisa, if I have foreseen your future right.' Grandmother wagged a finger at her and spoke sternly now.

'You must listen carefully because things have changed. That woman escaped to come home with tales of the countries of the east. But now the raiders take their captives west to the sea, and no one has ever returned to tell us about their fate.

'Strange men with pale skin and red hair came to the coast', she continued, 'and built great forts that were amazing to see. I think they are the sons of demons. When people are taken inside those walls, no one returns.' Grandmother shuddered. 'Perhaps they eat them. We don't know, but that is why it is so important never to be taken by those devils.' Grandmother spat that last word out with bitterness.

'Go home now, Kisa. It is not your fate to be eaten by the white devils, of that I am sure. I am tired now. Go home.' Kisa went, but not home.

She climbed high into the Sentinel Tree and thanked him for warning her.

'It . . . is . . . good,' the wind in the leaves whispered back to her.

Chapter 10

Aftermath

The next day, Chief Abrafo called a meeting. A count was taken, and weeping family members reported who had been kidnapped.

'Adisa, my Adisa is gone!' Esi sobbed in the arms of Afia, who was crying too. Kojo stood with his head down and fists clenched. All the memories of the loss of his mother flooded back in his mind.

'We will have to move the village,' Chief Abrafo declared. A groan went out among the adults, but at first, no one argued. They had been found. If they stayed, the raiders would return.

'I will miss my tree if we have to move,' Kisa told Kojo as they sat watching the adults make plans. 'We will find a taller one,' Kojo promised her. But Kisa answered, 'I don't think so. He is the king of trees in this forest. That is why I want to stay.' She kept her secret that the Sentinel Tree talked to her. It was a very private thing, and she did not wish to share it with anyone, even Kojo.

'That one they called Mbwana will be back,' Chief Abrafo continued the argument for moving. 'I have not seen him before. He is young, strong, and cruel. He will want more of our people.'

'I will have to stay and tend the crops anyway,' Thimba replied. 'You can stand with us and help feed our people, or you can run away and starve while we die defending our children's future if you do not help guard us.'

Chief Abrafo was silent. He bristled at the intimation that he was a coward. The people held their breaths. Would there be a fight? Then Grandmother stood up and stepped between the two warriors.

'We must eat, and we must hide. We can move the youngest, the mothers, and the elders deeper into the forest. We can make it look like everyone is still here. We can improve our defences and set traps. We must change the maze to make it harder to find. But we must harvest these crops so we can feed everyone for the next year. I see no argument here. We must do what we must to survive, and moving everyone to a new village is impossible. Cut the spear off the top of the Sentinel Tree. That will make us harder to find again.'

The obeah had spoken. Both men recognised the wisdom in her solution. Thimba sat down. He had no desire to challenge Chief Abrafo's leadership. Kisa breathed a sigh of relief that she would not have to leave her tree behind, and she did not think he would mind losing the spear of dead wood at the top.

Chief Abrafo raised one arm. 'So be it. Cut the top of the tree. The hunters will find a place for a more hidden village. Everyone else will work on the defences or the crops. We must be ready for this Mbwana when he returns.'

'I will do it!' Kisa called out. All stopped, stunned, and turned to look at the slim figure of the seven-year-old girl. Someone laughed at her and then fell silent under the glare of her eyes.

'I will help her,' Kojo found himself chiming in. 'We are light. Grown men are too heavy to climb so high.' Someone else started to speak, but Chief Abrafo raised his hand for silence as he looked at Kisa, as if seeing her for the first time.

'Yes,' said Grandmother. 'It will be so. Let she who loves this tree and understands its power do this.'

'But', Thimba interjected, 'she does not have the strength—'

'You do not know what she can do!' Grandmother turned to him. 'Give your daughter your axe. She will surprise you.'

Thimba removed a small axe that he used for cutting firewood from his belt and handed it to Kisa. She marched to the tree with it and began climbing one-handed with Kojo close behind. When they reached the base of the spear, Kojo asked if she wanted him to strike it, but she shook her head no, closed her eyes, and put her forehead against the tree.

'Forgive me, brother. I have come to take your spear away so that we can be hidden from the devils,' she whispered, and Kojo was surprised to hear the tree answer.

'Take . . . it,' a deep whisper came from the leaves. 'We give it to you gladly.'

Kisa straddled the branch and began chopping at the stem. To everyone's surprise but Grandmother, on the tenth stroke, a crack was heard, and shortly thereafter, the spear broke and fell heavily through the living branches to land with a thud on the earth.

No one touched it until Kisa and Kojo followed it back to the ground. Then Grandmother squatted beside it and said softly, 'It must be buried with honour and the proper rituals. But first, I will make a fetish from its bones for you, Kisa. It holds great power—the power of the trees—and it will serve you in time of need.' Chief Abrafo and Thimba and the others listened, not quite understanding, but seeing Kisa in a new light—the light of a new obeah being created before them.

The changes were not easy. The hunters explored the forest until they found a small clearing where new huts could be erected. A path was made, and days were spent carrying supplies to the new location and erecting huts. In-between times, the path was concealed with brushes and brambles. The new village was manned at first by a caretaker and his family and some of the elders. Other people came and went. Women came to give birth and tend the babies, but most had to return to the main village in order to help with the work. The new village was a good place to store extra food and valuables and to hide the weak, but the life of the people still centred around Kisa's Sentinel Tree.

Grandmother saw that the spear from the tree was properly buried. It was, after all, the sacrifice the tree had made to show them the way when lightning had struck it so long ago. As she had promised, she cut off one small piece, said the incantations to keep its power, and gave it to Kisa.

'Keep it with you always because the spirit of the tree is in that piece of wood. Even when you are far away from here, you can call on it to help you,' she explained, giving it to Kisa in a small cloth bag. Kisa took it with a sense of awe and used a string tied around her neck to keep the little pouch close to her heart.

The adults were busy from dawn to dusk, planting and tending crops or out hunting, but it was a hard year, and some of the smallest children died. The loss of manpower they had suffered and the destructive looting of more than half the village had a devastating effect.

Kisa watched Grandmother prepare the little bodies for burial, and she cried when they were laid to rest. 'Why do they have to die?' she asked. Grandmother could see she needed a story to comfort her.

'Back in the beginning, there was no death,' Grandmother began. 'All the people and animals lived forever. They did not know that the sky god was thinking about death. At first, he decided that death was a bad idea and that no one should die. He called Chameleon to him and said, "Go to the people and tell them they will live forever."

'Chameleon did as he was told, but he walked as you have seen him, slowly and with great care, moving only one foot at a time and stopping often to look before taking another step. So the journey was very slow.

'In the meantime, the sky god kept thinking about death and why it would be a good thing. "Bodies get old," he thought, "and need to be replaced with new ones." And so he changed his mind. He called Lizard to him and said, "Go tell the people that they will die."

'Lizard, like Chameleon, did as he was told. Now Lizard is very fast, and he ran so quick that he passed Chameleon and reached the people first. He told them that they were going to die. Later, when Chameleon arrived, he gave the people his message, but it was too late. The message of Lizard arrived first and could not be undone.'

Kisa looked sad, but Grandmother continued, 'But Mother Earth said, "My children will come back to me when they die, and in me they will live forever as the ancestors." And now that is so. These children that died, they had in them the spirits of the ancestors, and those spirits have returned to the earth to be reborn again someday. The cycle of life goes on, Kisa, and will never end.'

'But why is death good?' Kisa always had another question. Grandmother smiled. 'Because the body grows old, and you don't want to have an old body forever! Death is good because then we can get new bodies. Now go home, Kisa. This old woman needs to rest.' And Kisa went.

Kisa ran to look for Kojo. She understood about the sky god now, but she still blamed the man on the black horse for the deaths of the children. She hated him, and she wanted to kill him.

'I am going to kill that Mbwana man,' she confided to Kojo when she found him.

He laughed and told her, 'You should mind to women's business and leave the killing to me! That is men's work.'

That made Kisa angry. She pulled away from him and shouted, 'No! I am going to kill him! You wait and see!' And she stormed off.

Later, she told the old woman about her argument with Kojo while she watched Grandmother prepare herbs. She was pleased when the obeah agreed with her. 'Yes, child, when you are grown, you will be a great fighter. I have seen in my dreams that a man will come here from a strange land. He will be dark-skinned like us, but he will be dressed in strange clothes. He will teach you to fight, and then you can kill all the white devils.'

Kisa went back to the Sentinel Tree, holding her fetish tight. She was going to kill the evil ones who had attacked the village.

'You will . . . That is . . . your . . . destiny,' the wind in the branches whispered back, and she felt better. Kojo might not believe her, but the Sentinel Tree did.

Meanwhile, Grandmother decided it was time to get help. The raid had frightened her. Her spells and the work of the villagers to hide the village in a maze had been successful for so long that the raiders had surprised her. 'I was not watchful enough,' 'And my obeah skills alone will not allow Kisa to do what she must do,' she muttered over her favourite cup of herbal tea. It was time to find her a teacher of the arts of the warrior, someone who could teach her how to fight. Her dreams had shown her who to look for.

The old woman got up and began preparing a potion. She called to her assistant Abba to guard her till she awoke, and then she drank the bitter brew and lay down on her blankets. Her spirit animal, the tawny eagle, rose high above the world. On the eagle's wings she soared on the wind, higher and higher, until she could see all Mother Earth below her. The eagle spread its wings and glided while the earth turned beneath them. The fabled lands of Ind and Chin passed below her, and then she saw islands in a strange sea. One island called to her, and the eagle plunged towards the earth. In a house with a peaked roof, she sensed rather than saw a man sleeping. He was a strong tall black man though his hair was white with age.

'Listen to me, old man,' she called to him in his dreams. 'You must return home. I have a child who will be the mother of her nation. You must train her!'

Then the eagle rose high again, and the world turned until her own country was beneath her. The obeah woman returned to her body, exhausted but satisfied.

As Esi gave her a tea to drink, Grandmother mused to herself, *I will have to send him that message in a dream every night until he acts. But at least I know the way now.*

Far away on the other side of the world, Yasuki woke from a dream that he could not forget. It was such a strange dream that at first, he dismissed it, but it kept recurring night after night. He was old, and his first thought was that he had no desire to return to Africa. Then he realised that he wanted to see his home again and not die alone so far away. It was the long sea journey that he had no desire to repeat. He sighed. But the dreams would not go away.

One morning, after a particularly vivid version of the dream, he got up and put on his beautiful blue silk robe—a gift from his former master, the great shogun Oda Nobunaga. He sighed again. His master had lost his last battle and had been forced to commit seppuku, ritual suicide. He missed him, though that had meant freedom for the tall black samurai.

He remembered when he first met Oda. His Portuguese master, the Jesuit priest who had brought him here from Africa, had been forced to give Yasuki to Oda on the very first day that they arrived. There had been a riot at the docks when Yasuki stepped down the gangplank behind his master. They had never seen a black man in Japan before. To them, he was a giant, though at home his height had been normal.

Lord Nobunaga heard about the riot and ordered the priest and his servant be brought to him. He made Yasuki strip to the waist and scrub himself to prove he was not covered in black ink. Yasuki smiled at the memory. Oda told the priest to give Yasuki to him as a gift. It was the best day of his life. Oda trained him in the art of a samurai, made him his right-hand man, gave him this house, and over time, made him a very rich and respected man in Japanese society.

And now this old Obeah woman wanted him to return, to train this girl—not of the same tribe as him but of the motherland . . . Yasuki made up his mind. It was time to go home.

Sefu was having strange dreams too. After the raid and successfully selling his captives in the Portuguese stronghold, he had made his way back to his home town of Agadez, far to the north-east. There, resting in his comfortable quarters, which he had earned as the commander of his own raiding party, he woke each night from a dream that never varied. He saw the girl child in the tree. He chased her. Always she ran away from him. He could never catch her though he wanted to. Badly.

Chapter 11

Yasuki's Journey

Crossing the Indian Ocean was not as unpleasant as his journey to Japan. On the way over, they had sailed south to catch the wild winds of the roaring forties that carried ships quickly but not comfortably.

Yasuki hated that crossing, for he was being carried away from his home, his family, and all he had ever known. The ship plunged and bucked through the mountainous waves, and his Portuguese master, the Jesuit priest, spent the entire trip vomiting in his quarters. His master had a hammock, but Yasuki, whose name back then was Issufo, slept on the hard floor.

It was Issufo's job to clean up the messes and tend to his master's needs, but whenever he could, he escaped the evil-smelling room for the fresh air on deck. That meant putting up with the freezing winds, the icy salt spray, and the coarse, rude crew of the ship. His stomach was strong, but nothing else about the voyage was much of a positive. He did not like the sea, and his heart ached for his home.

On the return trip, the ship meandered through the tropical seas of the island chains south of Japan and then hugged the coast through the straits of Malacca, the Andaman Sea, and around Ind. The journey was much more pleasant, with calm seas and gentle winds. Many stops were made at interesting cities, filled with wondrous sights that, as a rich man, he could enjoy.

He travelled in luxury this trip instead of as a slave. He slept in the hammock instead of on the floor, and he had a room to himself, with his most prized and important possessions: his swords and armour, plus clothes of silk that he had made before he left. He also had a sizable stash of gold and silver to pay his way wherever he went. It could also be used to buy his way out of trouble and avoid the inconvenience of having to fight, but in fact, in his armour, with his lethal swords on his belt, he was a formidable figure who everyone respected and avoided.

Back to my Mother, he thought as he steadied himself against the pitch of the ship and gazed at the distant coast nearly a year after leaving Japan. He had never dreamed that he would return until the obeah woman came to him.

He walked down the gangplank to the docks and looked out over distant but familiar sights: black people everywhere, tall and proud, carrying their goods on their heads over ramrod-straight backs. He remembered his samurai training, when so many of the young Japanese men, so used to bowing before all their superiors, had to be trained to stand straight. But not Yasuki. His posture was perfect and added to the sense of being in the presence of a giant of a man.

He was not as quick as those little men, though he could beat them in all strength games. Even at his best they were more agile, but his long legs and arms gave him the advantage in sword fights and hand-to-hand combat. His agility was the first to slide with age, and he was now approaching his eightieth year, but his strength was still legendary among the samurai.

He was unknown here, but the crowds parted for him at the sight of the strange armour and swords. And though he was obviously rich, he was just as obviously not someone to be interfered with or easily parted from his wealth.

He bought a horse and a pack animal to carry all that remained of his worldly goods. He did not know where this obeah woman lived, but he was sure finding her was going to be a long journey. He intended to depend on his dreams to get him to her and the child.

He set off north, following ancient Swahili trade routes. Although languages changed with each village, all spoke Swahili as well. He passed through lush forest country, over endless plains, past tall mountains, until he came at last to the Sahel country south of the great desert.

He turned west and followed the ancient trading roads across the endless Sahel. He passed slave raiders, but they gave him a wide berth once they saw his armour and swords. They were looking for easier prey.

Each night when he slept, he dreamed. The old obeah woman guided him, telling him to continue west. 'Tamale,' she whispered. 'Turn south at Tamale.'

Chapter 12

The Mind of the Sorceress

The months after the raid were the busiest of Kisa's life. The twins were still babies, and Ama was able to do very little other than breastfeed them as the wounds of their birth slowly healed. And then there was Kisa's new position as an apprentice to the sorceress.

When Kisa finished her chores, she went to help Grandmother. Most days were spent tending the needs of the villagers, but Kisa's favourite days were spent in the forest. On those days, the old woman handed her baskets to carry and then, without another word, walked into the jungle with Kisa following.

As she walked, Grandmother's bare feet connected with the soil, the plants, and the roots of the trees. She noted every bird song, the noises of the small furred creatures, and the slithering or scampering noises of the cold ones. Her eyes, still sharp after unknown decades, flitted up and down, back and forth, looking for the mushrooms, herbs, flowers, roots, or shoots that she needed for her craft. Her fingers, still nimble and untouched by arthritis, picked what she needed and popped the pieces into Kisa's hands to place neatly in the baskets.

As she did, she spoke the name of each just once and then moved on. After several hours, Grandmother sat on her favourite spot, in the sunshine beside a trickling stream, and accepted a drink of water from Kisa. She fetched it with a small wooden bowl kept by the creek. After Grandmother,

Kisa also drank. Then they sat in silence until the old woman rose, and they headed back to the village.

'Fetch me a bowl of porridge, child. Then recite the names as you take the plants from the baskets.'

Kisa was prepared to do just that. The women often played naming games with the children when they got home from gardening and gathering. Kisa recited the names perfectly as she laid out the treasures.

'Can I learn magic too, Grandmother?'

'There is no such thing, Kisa.'

'What do you mean? I have seen you! You call demons and make fires burn in strange colours. You make men love girls after they visit you.'

Grandmother laughed. 'All of that is tricks, not true magic. Some of what I do calls on the spirit world to help us, and maybe that is magic. But people are easily fooled, and they believe what they want to believe. Much of what I do helps them believe in our stories, but it is not magic.'

Kisa looked disappointed. 'But how can I kill the slave raiders and the white devils if I don't have magic?'

'You will have much knowledge that you can use to fool them, for they are just as afraid of the spirits and as easily led as any other men. You will know the uses of the herbs of the jungle, and those will help you too. But it is your strength and the rightness of your cause which will defeat them in the end—not mere magic.'

Kisa did not quite understand, but she nodded thoughtfully as she thought about the mystery of Grandmother's words. Gradually, as her skills developed and her knowledge deepened, she saw the truth of the obeah's words. People believed what they wanted to believe, no matter how strange. With a few powders thrown in the fire, some chanting, and a potion, Grandmother could convince the people of almost anything.

And why not? She told them what they wanted to hear. She validated their beliefs and kept their world understandable and safe. Life was not easy, but the sorceress knew how to make the people feel safe, and sometimes that was all that was needed.

At the same time, Kisa could see how powerful Grandmother was and how important she was to the tribe. If she could not heal someone, they died. Her role was vital, even if most of her magic was only real to those who believed in it.

Grandmother had lived so long that all who saw her birth were gone, and so were many more far younger than she. Her mind was clear and sharp, though her hearing and sight had deteriorated. Her joints were stiff, but she stood straight and still tall. Her hair had been white far longer than it had been black. The wrinkles on her face were deep, like scars, marking the tracks of her tears, her smiles, and her anger.

Her anger could seem awesome to the youngest generation, but mostly what she felt was irritation—at their ignorance mostly and the arrogance that went with it in the young and foolish. She searched constantly among them to identify the strongest and smartest. And in these children, she placed a lot of her efforts and strength.

Kisa was the last, she knew. She had been waiting for Kisa for all her life in a way, though she did not know it until she was already old. She was born in the original village, on the edge of the great ocean from which both bounty and peril came.

Her childhood was lost in the mists of time, for she had to grow up quickly—too quickly. It was in her childhood that the Portuguese arrived on the shores of the cape, named it Cape Tres Puntes, and built the lighthouse that still shone brightly each night to warn the slave ships off the rocks, where they deserved to founder for their evil ways.

She remembered clinging tightly to her mother's hand when they came ashore in their long boats. She remembered how ugly they were, with long and dirty matted hair, scraggly beards, skin the colour of something rotting, and a smell to match. Never had she smelled anything as evil as the men from their ship.

They planted a flag and said some strange words. She only found out later that they were claiming the land for their king in Portugal. They took no more notice of the black people watching them than they would have if they had been animals. Grandmother spat at the memory. *They thought themselves superior then, and they think it now, but it is they who are the animals!*

Like many of the old, she did not sleep much at night any more. Everybody's problems weighed her down. She was as close as the village could come to a marriage guidance counsellor. Her counselling abilities came from years of practical experience helping couples keep the lifelong vows they had taken and helping people who were living in both isolation in the forest and yet having to live too close to their neighbours in a small village. Fights broke out. People became estranged. Families stood against other families.

It was a problem for every tribe of humans for over a hundred thousand years at least, given the archaeological evidence from Africa. The ancestors of the Buganda people were living in that rich land a hundred thousand years ago. The evidence is that the oldest cultures were matrilineal and acephalous, which means 'without a head of state'. In other words, no kings or queens, where adults were more or less equal in status, and this was the society that Grandmother lived in.

In this village, there was a chief, but his authority, like hers, was limited. But people respected the elders because without the elders, the knowledge of how to survive in a harsh environment would be lost.

So she worked tirelessly each day to both pass her knowledge on and to mediate between families in order to keep the harmony of the group, without which survival was not possible. She worried about pregnant women and spent long hours at night planning the deliveries of their babies and the pre- and postnatal-care needs of their mothers.

She spent many late hours of the nights lying awake under her blankets, while her assistants or charges snored peacefully on their mats. *Is Ekuba going to go into labour soon? Is Atu beating his wife? Is Ashahi starting her period? Should she marry Dia or Fela? Will there be enough food when the dry season comes?*

Thoughts and questions and never enough answers . . .

Around dawn, she dozed, dreaming strange, uncomfortable dreams from which she awoke exhausted. She didn't let that stop her. She was up before all others, tending the teapot and the porridge, thinking about the day's tasks—get everyone up, fed, and moving, then see the patients, anyone with a problem who was lined up outside her door. She was to teach her assistants, deliver a baby, or treat an illness. That often involved visits to other huts and long hours making medicines and treating people. If she had time, she took Kisa and went hunting for medicines.

Sometimes, in the heat of the afternoon, when the tribe had eaten their main meal and were resting, she had time to herself. She liked to move slowly around her hut, inspecting the earthen jars of herbs, insect parts, and other ingredients that she used in her medicines, but her mind was in the past. It was her escape—to remember the good times and the bad times and all the people now long dead. Sometimes, it was as if she were visiting with them. She shared with them her current problems and asked them what they would do—especially her teacher, the obeah woman before her.

When the tribe was forced to move inland to protect the people from the slavers, she was apprenticed to the obeah woman. She laughed at the thought of how scared she had been of that old sorceress. Now she was just like her, feared and respected by all but, in reality, just an old woman who was growing tired of the responsibilities and eager to pass on the job.

'Soon, soon,' she whispered to herself.

When she had the time to think, she liked to remember her travels the most, back in the days when everyone still knew her as Ashahi.

Her apprenticeship had been long, and her internship under the head obeah had been much longer. She had been Great-Grandmother's main assistant all through her twenties and thirties and into her forties. She had never married and never had children because she knew her calling was to replace the old obeah when she finally walked out of her body and into the spirit world. But by the time she was in her forties, Ashahi was restless. Perhaps it was because she had never had the fulfillment of children. She did not know, but she remembered how dissatisfied she had become. How irritable and—she had to admit now—how disagreeable.

Great-Grandmother noticed and called Ashahi to her one day. 'You are unhappy, my child. I think it is time for a change. The village has many things we need, and the chief has organised a trading party to take the blankets that the weavers have made and trade them for iron for new farm tools. You are strong. You can carry a load of goods yourself, and you can practice your healing skills if they are needed. It will be good for you. You have not left this village since you came here as a child.'

'But who will help you?' Ashahi was taken back by the idea at first, remembering her responsibilities.

'I have time left. I will look after the village until you return.'

She left her village with the traders and did not return for many moons. In that time, she wandered over many countries to the east and north along the trading roads. She learned several languages as well as the customs and bush medicines of many tribes.

Addo. Remembering her journey always brought back the piercing memory of the great love of her life. He was the leader of the trading party—his name meant 'king of the road', and he had been that: a proud, strong, and handsome older man whose wife had died and whose children were grown. Leading the trading parties was a perfect fit for him.

I was lucky that I was beyond childbearing by then, Grandmother thought. *But Dolphin Woman would never have allowed me to go if I could have. She must have known what would happen.*

It had been good for Ashahi to fall in love and have an intimate relationship with a good man. They were happy in the months on the road, and their relationship was accepted by their fellow travellers. He showed her the villages and the towns and took her to the marketplaces where he traded their mats and blankets for iron. He loved escorting her around, letting her try on lovely dresses and pretty jewellery. It had been so much fun.

I came back a better person, she thought. After that, her duties crowded in on her as Dolphin Woman suddenly became old and frail, and Addo went off on his trading journeys without her. From one of those journeys, he did not return.

Grandmother felt tears welling in her old eyes. *Enough!* she chided herself.

That was not what was important about her journey. What was important was that she saw for herself what was happening to the land and the people all around her, all the villages that were not protected by the maze and the magic.

She saw villages that had been stripped of their strongest men and women, living now with only the very old and the very young. She learned of the robed Arabs of the north who ran the slave trade that had plagued the motherland and her peoples for generations and who were now supplying slaves to the white devils, who were stripping even more people from the land of their birth, sending them on death marches to the sea, where they were sold and never seen again.

Her own people might irritate her now in her old age, but she saved her hatred for the white devils and the Arabs with their Swahili underlings.

So many stories that we will never hear again, songs we will never sing. So much that has been lost.

The obeah woman shook her head. There was no point in thinking about what had been lost. What was important was what could be saved.

We need a leader—someone to raise an army and throw them back into the sea.

CHAPTER 13

Evil Returns

When Kisa was ten, the slavers came back. She was teaching the twins, who now toddled along after her, how to climb her Sentinel Tree. Once again, the tree warned her, so she saw the slavers first. She screamed a warning and scuttled back down. She told the twins to go hide in the forest and then ran forward to help defend the village.

Sefu looked up at the tree and saw her, a beautiful young girl, not yet matured, perched high in a half-dead tree. A flash of memory came back: a girl child not six years old was there the last time, the child of his dreams. *The same!* he thought, as his eyes devoured the most beautiful female form he thought he'd ever seen.

His tastes were shaped by his childhood memory of his mother—tall and willowy; skin a rich chocolate brown; eyes large and dark; hair tight, black, and curly; long sensuous hands, fingers, and legs; and a slim body. Taut breasts, slim but still somehow very feminine. Lust rushed over him, and he gouged his spurs into his horse again. He forgot the rest of the villagers even though they were now moving towards him in a rough semicircle, armed with knives, short African swords, and farm implements.

'Take them!' he screamed at his lieutenants as his horse galloped through the line of the defenders and carried him into the village to the foot of the Sentinel Tree.

But she was gone. Her tree had whispered warnings to her of the coming danger. She in turn screamed out the warning to her people. As soon as she had given that call, Kisa leaped down out of the tree, grabbed a stick, and started running towards the raiders.

'What are you doing?' Kojo screamed and ran after her.

She ran faster, dodging between huts but heading relentlessly, stick held high, towards the raiders. Grandmother, coming out of her hut, saw her and yelled at her, 'Stop!' But Kisa was filled with a white-hot anger she had never felt before. All she wanted to do was kill that stranger on the horse, to put out the evil in those eyes, to beat him to death . . .

'Kojo! Stop her!' Grandmother screamed, and Kojo acted, putting on an adrenaline-fuelled burst of speed that enabled him to reach Kisa, grab her by the wrist, and stop her dead in her tracks. He was older, taller, and well muscled from both exercise and a flush of teenage male hormones, giving him a strength far beyond that of Kisa's ten-year-old girl's body. Her spirit was as strong as ten lions, but her body could not match it. Kojo clamped her wrist with one strong hand and began dragging her back through the huts and into the jungle.

Kisa's white-hot anger turned from Sefu to Kojo. 'Let me go! I have to kill him!' she screamed as she tried to pull free while digging in her heels. Kojo didn't look back. He just dragged her like a sack of yams with him deeper and deeper into the jungle. At last, he dived down into a gully filled with brambles and crouched down while fending off Kisa's stick, which she was trying to use to hit him.

He grabbed it, wrenched it out of her hand, and threw it away. Then he grabbed her other hand and held her till she stopped thrashing and screaming. When she realised it was useless to fight, she collapsed and began to tell Kojo that she hated him. Holding both of her hands in one of his, he put the other over her mouth, choking off her words. 'Hush!' he whispered urgently. 'You are not ready to fight them. Be quiet! If they find us, you cannot win against them! They will capture us or kill us! What good is that? Stop it, or they will hear us! We will fight them! We will kill them! But not today!'

He looked deep into her eyes as he said this, and she gave up. Cautiously he removed his hand from her mouth and freed one hand. She didn't move but looked at the ground and tried to control her ragged breathing. Kojo put his arms around her to protect her, and with a sigh she let him hold her.

Kisa looked around. The twins were beside her, having run to this ravine while Kojo was catching Kisa. She reached out and pulled them in close to Kojo. She spread her long arms and legs around the twins, pulling them in close to her so they would not be seen. Kojo put his head over them and wrapped his arms around Kisa. Then there was nothing they could do but wait, frozen, as still as their beating hearts and tortured breathing allowed.

They listened in silent fear to the shouts, screams, and fighting that seemed to go on forever.

Chief Abrafo and his fighters stood aside to let the big horse rush through, then they formed a line and faced the raiders. The twenty-odd hardened raiders with their two lieutenants with single-shot rifles were formidable foes. The first shots rang out over their heads to frighten and confuse them, but Chief Abrafo had heard guns before and countered it with a fearsome war cry that was taken up by the villagers as they met the raiders, knives against scimitars, sticks against whips and clubs.

The villagers held the line as best they could, but half the raiders dropped back and then spread out, leaving the lieutenants and the main body of raiders to keep the village fighters busy while they outflanked them, encircled them, and got into the village, where the most vulnerable prey were hiding in their huts.

Soon Chief Abrafo and his warriors were almost surrounded, fighting on three sides by warriors that could outfight them and were devilishly hard to kill. Eventually Chief Abrafo knew that he would have to order everyone to retreat in all directions, just hoping that the old and the young had time to get deep in the jungle and hide.

By this time, Sefu knew the girl was not in the village, and he was furious. He turned and began using his whip and sword to chase the remaining villagers towards the defenders. His lieutenants joined him. The pincers of his raiders were closing in, and Chief Abrafo gave the signal to disperse. Each villager then concentrated on breaking through the raiders and then running, leading them away from the most vulnerable.

Sefu stormed through the village as his raiders subdued the villagers who had not fled. He continued to look everywhere for the beautiful young woman he wanted so much, but he could not find her. 'Burn everything!' he called out to his men. 'Burn this shit heap and take everyone you can!'

He galloped in circles through the huts, hunting, hunting, while his men engaged the villagers and set fire to their huts.

Some of the villagers were captured, with each raider focused now on just catching one prisoner: getting someone down, knocking them out, getting shackles on them, then running to do the same to a second and a third. They were skilled at this job, and soon a group of captives was surrounded by three or four raiders while te rest turned back from the running defenders and began sacking the huts and looking for those who were trying to hide.

Chief Abrafo and his fighters were now trying desperately to make the raiders pay and to keep more victims from being captured. By the time they reached the edge of the village, half the raiders were forcing twenty-odd chained and screaming captives to move away, guarded on all sides by half the raiding party.

The other half were still sacking the huts and dragging their prey out to the retreating main party. Chief Abrafo and his men regrouped and managed to wound several of the raiders and kill two before the rest began retreating.

Sefu continued driving his big black horse in circles while his men sacked the huts. He used his whip on the defenders as they came back, all the while watching for any sign of the girl. He saw a tall man with scars on his arm holding off two raiders. He lunged forward and slashed the man with his whip. This gave his men the advantage they needed, and Thimba was taken.

The raiders obeyed their master. They torched the huts and put all the prisoners in chains. As the moon was rising, they left, driving their captives before them. Sefu followed, angry beyond words that the maiden had escaped him. The jungle swallowed up the raiders as quickly as they had come.

At last, in the quiet of the dawn, the children crawled out and back to the village. It was in flames. On the edges, the remaining people stood, stunned and silent, watching their homes disappear forever.

Kisa found her mother sobbing in Grandmother's arms. 'He's gone! Gone!' she was wailing. Kisa went cold with fear. Where was Papa? But deep in her heart, she already knew: her father was taken.

Older brothers and sisters came together with their children to grieve with her mother, but Kisa was wild with anger. She could not grieve for the anger that was welling up inside her.

Grandmother took her aside. 'I am glad you are angry. It shows your spirit. Someday you will avenge him.'

'I want to go now! I want to save him!'

'But you are not ready. If you go now, you will only be caught and enslaved yourself. That will not help your father. No, there is nothing you can do for him but this. You must become an obeah woman. You must learn from me all my arts and more. Then you can go forth and avenge your father.'

Kisa ran to the Sentinel Tree, tears blinding her eyes as she climbed higher and higher into his protective branches. 'He's gone, my father is gone!' she sobbed out her grief to her friend. The tree shivered, and the wind in the leaves sounded like crying. Her grief turned to anger. 'It's all Kojo's fault. He stopped me. I could have helped.' She stopped listening to the voices in the leaves. Her anger, when it burned hot, clouded her vision and her hearing.

When she finally came down, Kojo was waiting. He tried to comfort her, but she drove him away. 'This is your fault! I hate you! I never want to see you again!' She ran home, again in tears.

The remaining villagers were faced with the task of rebuilding the village. Again, they argued about moving the village. Again, it was easier to rebuild than move. The thatched roofs of the huts had burned, and so had the mats covering the doors and the blankets on the floor, but the sturdy mud-brick walls still stood. New thatch was made, and the men worked on the weaving looms whenever they were not in the gardens.

Kojo avoided Kisa or tried to placate her with small gifts. Sometimes he tried to help her with chores. She angrily refused all advances, even going so far as to spit on the ground at his efforts.

Finally, Grandmother decided that enough was enough and called Kisa to her. 'It is not Kojo's fault that your father was taken! I ordered him to catch you and take you to safety. What could you have done, you foolish girl? You would have been taken too, and then where would you be? You go to Kojo right now and apologise to him, or I swear I will take a stick to you!'

Kisa has never seen Grandmother so angry before. She didn't argue, but it still took a few days before her pride allowed her to do as she was told and apologise. As usual, Kojo was polite and accepted her apology. Kisa wished he would get angry back, but he refused to do that. She realised with a start that this was because he loved her. Somehow when her father was there, she never noticed. Now it was obvious.

Far away, Sefu was dreaming again. The girl child was now a beautiful young woman. He lusted after her and chased her, but he could never catch her. Each morning, he woke exhausted, having chased her endlessly without ever being able to catch her or satisfy himself.

In her village, Kisa was having matching dreams, so she went to Grandmother. 'That man, the slaver, is chasing me in my dreams. I don't like it. What should I do?'

'Call on your leopard spirit, of course,' Grandmother said impatiently, as if the answer was obvious.

'Oh.' Kisa thought about it. *Of course. The she-leopard!* She felt the strength of the leopard flow through her, as if she was looking in those great yellow eyes again. *When he comes back in my dreams, I will kill him!*

Chapter 14

The Sorceress's Apprentice

Kisa always wanted to learn more. Every day, she badgered Grandmother to teach her the skills she needed to fight the raiders.

'Patience. That is the first lesson. When you know all that I know, then you will be ready to learn more. Teachers will come. You will learn then the art of warfare. In the meantime, stoke the fire.'

'Today I will teach you the art of disguise,' the obeah began one day. 'Someday you will travel to faraway places that I cannot see. You will need to protect yourself by seeming to be what you are not.'

'How do I do that, Grandmother?' Kisa was eager to learn.

'It can be as simple as the clothes you wear. Always dress to fit in, wherever you are. You must learn to dress as a boy and seem to be a man. You must also be able to change your face, to look old or male or diseased. Strangers must never see you as you are, a young woman. No, you must practice how to walk and how to talk and how to use clothing to be seen as what you want them to see, not what you really are. Clothes are a start, but you must learn to use paints convincingly to conceal your true identity.'

Kisa couldn't wait to start mixing the pigments and experimenting. She practiced being male, being old, being diseased. She learned to paint scars and tattoos on her skin that looked real. She could make wrinkles so convincing that she looked older than Obeah. Dressed like a young man, she learned the cocky strut, the language, and the deeper voice. She learned to handle weapons as soon as she could grasp a stick; now she practiced the art of handling herself like a man.

'Now you must learn how to confuse the minds of those who come too close. I will teach you how to hypnotise people who get close enough to look into your eyes. They will be close enough to see through your disguises, but you will muddle their minds and give them thoughts—"I see a filthy peasant boy. I see a sick old woman." They will see whatever you want them to think they are seeing. And it will be.'

Kisa was excited. She enjoyed dressing up, acting, and painting herself into different roles, but this was different. This was magic at last! Oh, she knew how to make potions already, medicines and drinks that changed the way the drinker thought and acted. But this! *This is true magic,* she thought, as a shiver went up her spine.

Grandmother also taught her languages: Ashanti, Fante, and other local dialects. Later, she learned Swahili, Portuguese, and Dutch. Kisa was like a sponge when it came to new languages, so when Grandmother saw her abilities, she taught her as much as the old obeah woman remembered from her long life.

Grandmother's lessons in hypnosis were put into practice with everyone she met. If someone were to get too close and begin to guess at the truth, she learned all the skills to ensure that she could change their minds and set them on a different path. Putting them to sleep was the easiest, changing their memories was harder, making them do something they would not normally do depended on how easy they were to hypnotise, but luckily most people were easily led.

The knowledge of the old obeah woman was vast and varied. From the time Kisa was very young, Grandmother taught her the words in different languages—Nzema first, then Ashante, the language of their nearest powerful neighbours, the Ashanti Kingdom.

But Grandmother knew the ability of the very young to absorb several different languages at once. By this time, Kisa was fluent not just in those tongues but also knew some of the Ga people's language and the closely related Hausa tongue of the Niger country.

Grandmother also taught her two of the important languages to the north of the forest country—dialects of the languages spoken by the Dagbani tribes such as the Dagomba and the new language of the Songhai invaders of the savannah country, the Gonja horsemen, and traders.

By the time she was in her teens, Kisa was speaking four major languages and several dialects as well, and Grandmother had kept her own skills in those languages by teaching her. Daily they spoke to each other in half a dozen different tongues, shifting back and forth as they went through their daily chores.

Grandmother continued to pass on her botanical and substance knowledge as well. Her understanding of local plants was encyclopedic. She knew the names, uses, and dangers of them all and in several languages. Kisa had to continue learning the uses and preparation methods on a daily basis and then help Grandmother decide which medicines or potions were called for in the daily life of the tribe. And there were no books to refer to. The knowledge had to be in the heads of the users and passed on to the next generation in order not to be lost.

Kisa was not Grandmother's only apprentice. There were other girls who were learning, especially the skills of midwifery and women's medicine. But with Kisa, Grandmother was concentrating on survival skills, from 'magical' tricks that could get her out of tight spots or convincing doubters of her powers, herbs that would heal wounds, hypnosis and disguise, and sleight-of-hand tricks that could get her what she needed.

Chapter 15

The Black Samurai

One bright day, Kisa was climbing the Sentinel Tree when the wind in the leaves turned to words: 'Someone comes!'

'Is it slavers?' she asked. The leaves rustled in confusion. 'No danger,' they whispered, but there was an uncertainty too, as if the tree was confronting someone altogether new.

She looked out and saw a stranger walking up the path, tall and black as night, with skin much blacker than her own chocolate-brown colouring. He was dressed in clothes different from any she had ever seen before. He had a quilted jacket with strange pads on the shoulders. Across his stomach were pieces of leather attached to his jacket by metal studs. The white designs running down the black jacket sleeves were strange too—symbols of an unknown language perhaps.

He carried two swords in the belt at his waist. Their hilts were nothing like the hilts of the short swords her people used, and they were long, slim, and curved in their black scabbards. Instantly she wanted to see them.

She was stunned by his strange and dangerous look that yet somehow felt safe to her. She was sure that he was coming to help her and that her enemies were his. He was obviously dangerous to people like the slavers, but she knew he would never harm her, would in fact be willing to die for her. He looked fit and strong, but Kisa also knew somehow that he was as old as Grandmother.

At last she called down the signal that a stranger was approaching. Instantly the villagers sprang into action—children scurrying out of sight, men and women gathering together and looking in the direction that Kisa was pointing, with their farming implements, knives, and swords casually held in resting positions but visible to the approaching stranger.

The stranger walked out of the trees and halted in plain sight but out of the reach of arrows. He planted his staff in the soil, which was also a spear from the look of the jagged but well-formed metal on the top.

'Greetings,' he said in perfect Nzema. 'I wish to speak to your obeah woman.' He was looking straight at Kisa, behind the adults, now halfway down her tree and sitting comfortably on a large limb, her long legs swinging gently as she looked back straight into his eyes.

Grandmother moved forward, and the villagers moved aside for her. Two men flanked her for protection as she walked up to the stranger. Just out of reach of that deadly spear, she stopped and said, 'Then it is I whom you wish to speak. You are welcome here if you mean no harm to my children,' and with a gesture, she showed she meant everyone behind her.

Kisa jumped down when Grandmother moved forward and was now at the head of the crowd. Her eyes were still fixed on the stranger's. He bowed gracefully to Grandmother, but his eyes too were fixed on Kisa.

'Thank you for your welcome. I mean you no harm. I had a vision of a great sorceress who would rise against the white devils. My vision led me to you, for I believe you are entrusted with her care and education.' Now he looked hard into the eyes of the ancient obeah woman in front of him. She met his eyes with steel in hers.

'Perhaps it is so. How does this concern you?'

'I have been to the far side of the world, to a country so strange that you cannot imagine it. I learned their art of fighting, which is so strong that, even though I am old, I can defeat any warrior here. After my master died, I had a strange and powerful dream that brought me back to my homeland. I have followed that dream across our motherland till today I stand before the object of my dreaming.'

He turned to Kisa and knelt on one knee. 'Let me serve you, my queen. And teach you.'

Kisa walked forward as if in a dream and placed her hand on his head. 'I accept your service. Rise,' she heard herself say. She stepped back, and he stood up.

The villagers were confused by what just happened. To them, Kisa was a snip of a girl, nothing much. Grandmother had not shared with them her foreknowledge of who she was or what she could become. Grandmother moved swiftly now.

'Come,' she said with authority as she turned back to the village. 'We will talk over cocoa. You must be tired from your journey.' She took Kisa by the arm and firmly marched her back to the obeah's hut, with her bodyguards and the stranger right behind her. The guards stopped at the entrance, and the stranger was shown inside.

He took off his strangely made sandals and left his spear at the door. The swords remained on his belt as he sat down on the mat before the fire, where Kisa was serving up the hot cocoa. Grandmother seated herself facing him and waited patiently while he drank before questioning him.

'What is your name? Where are you from? Where did you go on the other side of the world? Tell me your story,' she said at last.

'My birth name was Issufo, but for many years now I have been known as Yasuki, the Black Samurai,' he began. Grandmother and Kisa listened to his story without interruption though it took till dark to tell.

'I was born a long time ago in a country called Mozambique by our Portuguese masters. My people are the Makua and have been in that land since before time began. I was the servant of a Jesuit priest, Alessandro Valignano, who was sent across the ocean to inspect the Jesuit missions in the East Indies in 1579. It took us two years to reach the country of Japan, and we reached the capital in the spring of 1581.'

He chuckled. 'I caused a riot. I know now that they'd never seen a black man before, and although I am not that tall a man in my home, I towered over these short yellow-skinned people. Several people were crushed to death just trying to get a look at me.

'The local lord heard the noise while he was praying at the temple and ordered that my master and I be brought to him. He thought I was dyed with black ink, so he made me strip to the waist and scrub my skin! He made an offer for me. My master reluctantly accepted in order to maintain good relations with these people, and I entered my lord Nobunaga's service.'

Yasuki took a sip of his drink and sat silently for a few minutes before continuing. 'He had me trained in the martial arts of the samurai. I learned to fight with my body, my swords, and any other weapon in hand. I served him very well for many years as his weapon bearer. I was a rich man there, with my own house.

'Then, my lord Nobunaga was attacked and forced to kill himself in Kyoto by the army of their leader, Akechi. I was also there and fought the Akechi forces. Immediately after my lord's death, I joined with his son. I fought alongside him for a long time, but eventually I had to surrender my sword to Akechi's men.

'They asked Akechi what to do with me. Akechi said that a black man was a beast and did not know anything, so they should not kill me but take me to the temple of the southern barbarians, the Jesuit church. I think Akechi spoke that way about me to save my life. He gave them a reason not to kill me. The Japanese did not hate me or think of me as a beast. Indeed, they admired me because I looked like their god, whom they called the Buddha. Many of his statues showed him with black skin. Or perhaps Akechi did not want to offend the Jesuits, needing all the friends he could get. In any case, they took me to the Jesuits, who praised God for my safety.

'I lived quietly after that until I began to have dreams.' Yasuki looked directly at Grandmother as he said this, and a smile darted across her lips. 'So I returned to Africa. I did not think I would ever return, but here I am. Mother Africa wants me to teach this girl all that I know so that she may free the Mother's children of the scourge of the white devils.'

Grandmother nodded at the end of the tale. 'I will see that you have food and shelter provided to you. You must also teach her companions, for she cannot do this job alone.'

Kisa was beside herself with excitement, but she kept it bottled up. She showed Yasuki to his new home and brought him food, water in a pot, and anything else that he needed for his new life in her village.

Then she went in search of Kojo and the twins, who couldn't wait to hear about the strange old man they saw arrive. Breathlessly, she repeated his story almost word for word and then finished with 'He is going to teach us how to use those swords! And the spear! And he said he will show us how to disarm and kill men with our bare hands too!'

Training had to wait till Yasuki was introduced and accepted by everyone. There were courtesies and rituals to be performed before he was considered a member of the tribe. The children waited through it all with great impatience, but the day finally came when their training began.

Much to the disappointment of the children, training began with lots of exercises and no swords. Yasuki expected them to run and jump, do endless push-ups and sit-ups, and listen to lessons on rules and respect. They chafed at the discipline, but gradually Yasuki shaped his raw recruits into a solid group of prospective warriors who understood the importance of following orders, and then the real training began.

After Yasuki's arrival, he began to teach Kisa and Kojo primarily, with the much younger twins, Shani and Kwame, watching. Then, as Kisa and Kojo learned the basics, Yasuki had them teach the twins, and gradually they too were able to join in Yasuki's lessons.

The other children in the village were at first curious and then jealous of the training that was happening in front of them. Yasuki solved that problem by telling Kisa and her companions to pass his knowledge on to the other children. He would not train them himself, but by teaching the other children, Kisa, Kojo, Kwame, and Shani were practising and honing their own skills.

'There is no better way to learn than to teach,' he finished. Grandmother nodded in agreement, and the next day, Kisa informed the rest of the children that they could learn from her if they wanted. They most certainly did, and soon the adults were joining them, when their chores allowed. Chief Abrafo thought it beneath his dignity to learn from children, but when he saw Kojo's growing skills, he changed his mind and began to learn the effective new techniques as well.

Chapter 16

Other Dreams

Once Yasuki reached Kisa's village, his nights were undisturbed by dreams. If he did dream, he did not remember them when he awoke. Grandmother too slept better now that the object of her dream searches had finally found them.

Kisa, however, was beginning to have dreams of her own, and in all of them, Kojo featured. He was growing into a strong and handsome young man who was always warm and caring to Kisa. She found herself wanting him to go a step further. In her dreams, he held her in his arms, and when she awoke, it was with a strange feeling deep in her stomach at the thought of his strong, lean body so close to her.

Kojo was also having dreams. Every night, he held Kisa in his arms and told her how much he loved her, how he had always loved her. Then he touched her all over until he awoke in a sweat.

At training the next day, Kisa and Kojo found it hard to look at one another. Shyness was not a natural state for Kisa, but suddenly the presence of Kojo caused her to look away and forget whatever it was that Yasuki was asking her to do. Kojo, on the other hand, was as clumsy as a child whenever he felt Kisa's eyes on him.

Yasuki noticed and spoke to Grandmother, 'These two are in love. It is making it hard for them to concentrate.'

Grandmother nodded. 'It is time for me to speak with them.'

She called Kisa to her first. 'You know you have a great destiny, Kisa. All the hopes of our people rest with you. Nothing must interfere with your training or that destiny—'

'I know, Grandmother,' Kisa interrupted. 'I train hard every day and—'

'And dream every night about Kojo,' Grandmother interrupted back.

Kisa's mouth dropped open. 'How . . . how do you know that?'

'How would I not know it? You should see yourself around him. You look away. You flutter your eyes. You have all the signs of young love. And why not? If you were any other girl, we would be preparing you for your marriage. Kojo would be a perfect husband for you. But it cannot be.'

Tears rose unbidden in Kisa's eyes. She clenched her fists and willed the tears away.

'Do you know why, my child?' Grandmother hadn't called her that in years, and her voice was uncharacteristically soft.

'Because you cannot get pregnant. How can you fight the slavers if you are carrying a child? You cannot do both. You can give up your destiny and become a wife and mother, or you can remain true to yourself and give up Kojo.'

'How can I give him up? I love him!' Kisa wailed.

'I did not say you could not love him. You don't have to give up that love. That, I think, will last forever. But you cannot marry him or come to his bed. It is that which you will have to do without. And you cannot trust your emotions. If you let him hold you, you will give in.'

'Never!'

'Then do as I say. Stay strong. Don't wish him to touch you.'

Kisa could take no more. She turned and ran from the hut and into the forest.

Kojo saw her go. Grandmother stepped out of the doorway and motioned him to come inside. He wrestled with the desire to chase after Kisa and then reluctantly followed Grandmother into the darkness.

The darkness grew stronger as he listened to Grandmother's words. He must not touch Kisa. He must not make love to her. He could not marry her—ever. She was willing to make that sacrifice, and so must he.

He did not argue. He knew Grandmother was right. But his loins ached at the thought of Kisa, his beautiful Kisa, always being out of reach. It wasn't fair.

'Nothing is fair, Kojo. Life is hard and will only get harder for you two. But our people need Kisa, and she needs you. Not as a husband but as the man who is always behind her, willing to die for her if necessary. Can you understand that?'

What Kojo could not understand was how Grandmother always knew what he was thinking, but he nodded, clenched his hands into fists, and turned to go.

'Go to her now, Kojo. Talk to her. Let her talk. Work it out between you how it will be. How it must be,' Grandmother said to his retreating back.

It wasn't hard to find her. She was hiding in a gully close to the village, but he could hear her crying. She was hunched up, her head in her arms. Kojo had not seen her cry since the terrible day her father was taken. Without a word, he gathered her into his arms.

She threw her arms around his neck, and for several minutes, they clung to each other in love and despair. 'I love you,' they said simultaneously, and then both of them were crying as they hugged one another.

Hours later, they returned to the village, hand in hand. They had talked and talked, pouring their hearts out to one another and vowing to love each other forever. They knew there could be no physical relationship, though they had been too shy to put that into words. But they also knew that neither would ever love anyone else. They were a team, whether married or not.

The next day they went back to training. Kisa no longer felt shy. Kojo no longer stumbled. They were totally focused now on what they had to do. Yasuki was satisfied.

He set Kojo and Kisa down together away from the others and said, 'One's duty in life is your responsibility to your highest self. This level of duty carries with it the requirement that you never do anything that is contrary to your true self. For a warrior, war against evil, greed, cruelty, and hate is the highest duty. If you do not fight this battle of good against evil, you will fail in both your worldly duty and in your duty to your higher selves. Not doing the right thing when it is required is worse than doing the wrong thing. Ordinary people strive to preserve their lives, but the warrior has a different way. Warriors must be ever ready not merely to safeguard others but to sacrifice their lives for a cause. That is what I expect from you. Nothing less.'

Kisa and Kojo sat up straighter. They were warriors. This was their calling. Whatever sacrifice was necessary in their personal lives, they were prepared to do it. It did not change their love for one another. That would never change.

Far away, someone else was dreaming about Kisa. The dream was always the same, and at first, he enjoyed it: the slim young girl in the tree smiling at him, him drawing closer and trying to catch her. Her running away laughing and disappearing, him growing hot and aroused but never any satisfaction. But now the dream was taking a dark twist. Instead of running away from him, she turned on him, and when she did, she became a leopard, with bright yellow eyes and slashing claws. The tables turned, and he had to run away from her. He hated that!

Sefu woke in a sweat and cursing. What was it about that girl that made him dream about her night after night?

Women were cheap and plentiful, but the only woman he wanted was a slip of a girl he had seen in that tree all those months ago. He cursed his decision to burn the village. It meant that they would have moved, making it harder to find. He was going to find her though. Only having her in the flesh would stop these dreams, of that he was sure.

Chapter 16

Students of the Samurai

Yasuki and Grandmother watched as the central gathering area around the Sentinel Tree became the village training ground. 'The slavers will find we have grown teeth,' Grandmother said.

In the months and years that followed, Yasuki drilled them in every art that he knew. He expected absolute obedience from all of them, including Kisa. She was the student, and he was the teacher, regardless of who she would become in the future. She and Kojo had to call him by a strange name: Sensei. He told them it was Japanese for *teacher* and a sign of the respect he had earned.

The young people were already fit from life in the village and a lean but nutritious diet. They flourished under Yasuki. First, Yasuki started with the rules. 'At the start of each practice, you must bow to me as the sensei and then to each other. It is a sign of respect and to show that you are friends and will not hurt one another, no matter how hard the fight.'

Yasuki always practiced these strict codes of conduct. Each day the students began by bowing to him, and in turn he bowed back but not quite so deeply. He taught them to bow to each other before each practice session in order to remember that their partners were their friends, not enemies. He taught them that they should always bow to their teachers and to never hurt anyone of a lower ability than themselves unless that person was hurting others.

He started with the philosophy behind the art of combat. 'There is the soft and the hard, the yin and the yang,' he began. 'Attack is hard, masculine. Defence is the yin, the yielding. It seems weak, but if correctly used, it can defeat the strongest yang, the strongest attack.'

Then he began to teach them the basics of hand-to-hand combat: how to punch and kick and, most importantly, how to block the blows of others. 'You can fight all day if you can always deflect the aggressor,' Yasuki told Kisa when she couldn't see the point of blocking. She just wanted to go in kicking and punching and get it over with.

'No,' Yasuki admonished her. 'You must be able to defend first. Defence is more important than offence. Defend, defend, defend, and then, when you see your enemy's weakness, strike. Strike hard, strike once, and you need never strike again.'

But at first, all the moves were practised alone. Kisa wanted to practice with Kojo and the others, but Sensei made them repeat the moves over and over in patterns of three: block, kick, block or punch, block, kick until all the moves were automatic. He only had to sing out 'Block, punch, block', and the students executed three perfect moves.

Kisa thought that would mean they could spar now, but no, Yasuki went on to complicated patterns where the three moves were coordinated with changes of direction, as if one were fighting opponents from all sides. 'These patterns are called kata', he informed them, 'and are important because seldom will you be facing a single enemy. You must be able to defend and attack from all directions at once.' And so the drills continued until Kisa thought they would never ever get to the real fighting.

But at last, one day, Yasuki had Kisa face Kojo. 'Bow to one another,' he commanded. 'Now you will practice with each other. But we will use the patterns we have learned. Kisa, I will tell you what three moves to use on Kojo. Kojo, you will step back as she approaches and block them. Then we will reverse it, and Kojo will attack.'

The others watched as Kisa and Kojo practiced, and soon all were taking the next step to actual fighting. Finally, months later, Yasuki allowed them to spar with each other.

Kojo was the better defender, Kisa soon found. She always went in strong, hitting and kicking as hard and fast as she could. Kojo, with a grin, never attacked himself but never let her get in a single blow. It was so frustrating to her, but the day he got in the first hit enraged her. She came in twice as hard after he kicked her hard in the gut, but she never touched him. He just went back to dodging and blocking, with that infuriating grin on his face.

Exhausted at last, Kisa bent at the waist, resting her hands on her knees and gasping for breath. To add insult to injury, though Kojo had not hurt her, Yasuki came over and clapped Kojo on the back, then lifted his arm into the air and declared him the winner of the fight.

'How can he be the winner?' she couldn't help but protest. 'I struck many times. All he does is defend!'

'But if it had been a real fight, he could have killed you with that one kick. Nothing you did touched him. He is the clear winner.' Yasuki turned and strode away, argument over. Kojo had the decency not to grin. Instead he went back to practicing his kata.

Kisa finally stood up and, breathing deeply, controlled her anger. She climbed high into the Sentinel Tree and thought long and hard about it. *If that is how to win, then I will do it Kojo's way,* she decided as she came down and began practicing the blocking kata.

Yasuki noticed but said nothing when Kisa adopted the same strategy, and the two danced around each other without advancing. At last, out of boredom, Kojo began throwing kicks and punches to liven things up. Soon Kisa did the same but softly and without charging in—a kick here, a sudden knife-handed strike there, looking for openings, looking for the chance to even the score.

It came with a manoeuvre that took her behind Kojo just long enough to land a punch to his kidney. It hurt, and he showed it. Kisa threw her hands in the air and shouted in triumph, 'I win!' Yasuki shook his head at such a show of pride and walked away. Kisa was crestfallen. Kojo was holding his side, but that big grin was back. She felt like slapping his face but knew he would block it, so she walked off after Yasuki.

'Why didn't I win?' She demanded to know. 'He won when he hit me!'

'But he did not hurt you. He only winded you. It was a controlled kick. Yours lacked control. You hurt him. Did you bow and apologize?'

Kisa closed her mouth. She had not even noticed that she hurt Kojo.

'Your blows must be so accurate that your opponent knows you could have hurt him but you didn't. You stop just one hair's width from actual harm. When you get a blow in to Kojo that shows me you could have hurt him but did not, then I will declare you the winner. Not before.'

Back to her tree, she went to think about this. 'He's right,' the leaves whispered.

She went back to training with one goal in mind. Get a proper blow in on Kojo—something that showed her ability to hurt him without doing so. Just like his kick to her stomach. It took weeks because Kojo was smart, cunning, and becoming a supremely good fighter.

She got a blow in one day when Kojo was feeling off colour and not as alert as he normally was. That took some of the pleasure out of it for Kisa, but nonetheless Yasuki did as he promised and lifted her arm up, declaring her the winner of that bout.

Kojo congratulated her, but she said, 'It never would have happened if you had been yourself. You are the better fighter, Kojo.' It was a hard thing to say, but she made herself say it.

'The fighting I do will always be for you, Kisa,' Kojo declared.

After a year of training, Yasuki made rough rope belts for Kisa and Kojo. 'You have passed the first level,' he said. 'Wear these belts in honour of your new skills but know that you still have much to learn.'

Far away, at home in Agadez, Sefu's dreams were becoming less pleasant. Night after night, he saw Kisa in his dreams, but the dreams were becoming nightmarish. She never smiled now, and instead of disappearing, she turned on him and attacked him. She stabbed him, and he woke with stabbing pains in various parts of his body. Always he tried to catch her, but when he approached, her eyes went fiery like that of a devil, and she hurt him. He began to fear the dreams and took to keeping women, either whores or slaves, with him at night so that he was not alone.

He began to fear the dreams. They were more than annoying; they were frightening somehow even though she was only a girl.

I'm tired of going west. It's been a long time since I went east. I wish to see Zanzibar again, he thought, though the real reason was to try and leave the dreams behind. He took only a small party of raiders with him, just enough to capture enough slaves to fund an extended visit to the fabled city. Sefu was more interested in partying than working these days. Anything that helped him escape from these dreams seemed preferable right now, and for some reason, they got worse when he was raiding villages.

The days passed swiftly for Kisa. Twice a day, she trained with Yasuki and her three companions. The afternoons were spent passing the knowledge on to the others with vigorous practice sessions. The rest of the day was spent helping Grandmother and gathering more information from her that could be useful in the coming battles.

Grandmother concentrated on the herbs and potions that could be used to maim or incapacitate her enemies. Kisa learned to mix sleeping potions, hallucinogens, and concoctions to make a person vomit blood or have an epileptic fit or some other equally dangerous effect on their health.

When their sparring was finally as perfect as he could make it, Yasuki began their weapons training. He helped them carve wooden knives and short swords. 'So you cannot hurt each other!'

Grandmother told Kisa when she protested at having to use wood. 'Be sensible. He is the teacher, not you. I want to hear no complaints from now on. He came from across the world to teach you. If it is too slow for you, grit your teeth, be silent, and train more! Now go. I have more important things to attend to than your impatience.'

Kisa gritted her teeth and went.

A few months later, Kisa got the chance to use her training for the first time in a real situation. Shani's best friend, Esi, had an abusive father who regularly beat her mother. It was between husband and wife, and so the tribe ignored the abuse, but it angered Kisa to hear the shouting in the mean little hut and then the screaming as the man beat his wife. But the day he hit Esi and then chased her out of the hut trying to hit her again was too much for Kisa.

She stepped between the two of them. The man stopped dead in surprise. 'Get out of my way!' he said with his fist raised. Kisa said nothing, but her right fist shot out and landed a perfect backhanded blow to the bridge of his nose.

He crumpled, seeing stars, as blood spurted out of his nose. Esi looked on in stunned silence. People gathered around. Esi's father crouched on the ground, cursing Kisa. Chief Abrafo arrived and demanded an explanation.

'He was hitting Esi. She is smaller than him. I stopped him before he hurt her.' Kisa said it impassively and stared straight ahead.

Chief Abrafo looked at Esi's swollen face and then at her father. 'Bring this to the village meeting,' the chief demanded. A meeting was called. Anyone who wanted to speak had the chance to do so. Esi's father railed about Kisa hitting him. Esi and her mother told the meeting about his violence. His family defended him. The family of Esi's mother defended her. There was much toing and froing until everybody had the chance to have their say.

Then Chief Abrafo asked the gathering as a whole for a judgement. The majority believed that Esi's father was in the wrong and that Kisa had acted honourably in the defence of Esi.

'The matter is settled!' Chief Abrafo declared. To Esi's father, he said, 'This violence against your family must stop. You are a man. Control your temper!'

He turned to the tribe. 'Go home now. It is time for the evening meal.'

As they moved away, he turned to Kisa, who had been joined by Yasuki. 'She did no damage to him,' Yasuki said as he looked in disgust at Esi's father. 'I have taught her well.'

The chief nodded and walked off. From the moment of Yasuki's arrival, he understood that Kisa was more than just Grandmother's successor. He watched the training with great interest because he needed warriors to defend his village, and this was an unprecedented event to have such a teacher come and turn his best and brightest youngsters into warriors. He didn't like Esi's father, being of the opinion that a true man did not hurt women, but he was also pleased that Kisa had shown such restraint and only broken the man's nose.

For a long time, they practised with wooden swords. At last, Yasuki sat them down and told them, 'Your sword represents your soul, so it is important that you make your own swords. We will use the wooden hilts of your practice swords and attach the steel blades to them.' Part of each day was then dedicated to making their own weapons: swords, knives, bows, arrows, and spears.

Kojo was best with the bow, and Kwame found he liked hand-to-hand combat best. Shani excelled with the long spear in one hand and a knife in the other. Kisa excelled at all the arts, but she was particularly adept with those strange long swords of the samurai.

It turned out even Yasuki had a magic trick or two up his sleeve, though he mostly left the magic to Grandmother. One day, he brought eggs to his students and showed them how to blow out the contents, leaving the eggshell empty. Then he took out a bag of red powder. 'This is called pepper. It is grown in the Far East and is worth more than gold to some.' He poured some of it in each of the four eggs.

'Keep these safe. If you are in hand-to-hand combat and need the advantage, smash this in the eyes of your opponent. It will blind him long enough for you to finish the fight!' The twins looked doubtful, so Yasuki blew a tiny bit of powder in Kwame's face. Kwame started sneezing violently and rubbing his eyes. 'It burns!' he cried as he ran to the washing bowl. Yasuki laughed. 'In the future then, do not doubt me.' And they never did.

There were so many things to learn. Yasuki knew military techniques, and he taught them all he knew about guerrilla warfare. 'You must never confront your enemies in open battle. There are not enough of you for that. You must learn the art of ambush, of sabotage, and of hitting them hard from behind and then disappearing again into the forest. And if you must fight, always be prepared to die.'

'But no!' Kojo protested. 'I want them to die. Not me.'

'It is bushido, the way of the warrior,' Yasuki countered with a smile. 'No one wants to die, but the god of the samurai, the Buddha, taught them that life continues after death in one form or another and that your life's choices are influenced by your karma.'

The young people looked blank.

'Karma is a law. Whatever you do comes back to you. If you do good, then good will come your way. Do wrong, and you will suffer for it. Not just in this life but in many lives. You do not know what will happen because of your karma. You think you will be successful, but this day, you may face your own death instead. You must always be prepared for that. Be prepared to die, and you will face down all the terrors that are thrown at you. If you fear death, you will become unable to move, unable to act. No one ever won a battle like that. Conquer your fear of death, and no enemy can stand before you.'

Kojo and the twins shook their heads in doubt, but Kisa knew it was true. Death did not strike any fear in her. She felt immune, invincible. 'I will conquer death. I will live until all slaves are free!'

Far away, in the great slave-trading city of Zanzibar, Sefu's dreams took a turn for the worst. Night after night, Kisa returned to haunt him. Now she carried a sword, and he had to fight her off to try and prevent her from killing him. Her sword always seemed to find his heart, and he awoke, clutching his chest, feeling the pain.

He went east instead of west because he was beginning to fear Kisa instead of just lusting after her. Sefu tried to rid himself of the dreams by indulging in all the women he could mount, accompanied by every other pleasure available. Alcohol, forbidden in Agadez, was freely available here. So were more exotic drugs from the Far East. But opium only made the dreams worse, and the women and alcohol worked not at all.

Chapter 17

New White Devils

In 1637, after several attempts, the Dutch took Elmina Castle from the Portuguese. One reign of terror seamlessly melded with the next.

For the most part, Kisa's village was cut off from the doings of the outside world. But in that year, a runner came breathlessly through the village with the news that different white devils now lived in the great Elmina slave castle.

'The Dutch have seized the castle. They have driven out the Portuguese. May the gods curse them both.' The runner was eager to share his news after a drink of fresh water and the promise of a feast in his honour.

There was confusion on the faces of most. The runner was patient and explained it to them. 'The Portuguese come from one part of the land to the far north of the world where the water turns to snow in the winters.'

There were more blank looks, but the runner pushed on. 'The people who live there speak many languages like we do, but they all have skin the colour of a dead fish's belly and some have hair that is yellow or red.' Most of the villagers nodded at that. They remembered Grandmother's stories about the white devils, but it had happened before most of them had been born, and none of them had seen anyone whiter than the Arab/Swahili raiders.

'These new people are lighter skinned than the Portuguese and speak a different language, and many of them have red hair. They have attacked the castle before many times, but the Portuguese threw them back. They come from a land called Holland, and they call themselves Dutch. Now the Dutch are the rulers, and they too want captives. It is said that the man who took the castle has also taken the land across the sea from the Portuguese. They want more slaves for their sugar plantations.'

'What is sugar?' Kojo asked.

The runner looked down his nose at such an ignorant question. 'It is a white powder that the white men love to eat. Maybe that is what turns their skin white. They use our people to work in the fields because they are so strong. Do you people know nothing out here?'

Chief Abrafo bridled at the insult, but Grandmother interjected, 'We know enough to stay as far away from the white devils as we can. Portuguese or Dutch—they are savages, devils in human form, and none of us here is stupid enough to want to work in their fields so they can make their white poisons.'

'Still you must know something of what is happening if you want to survive,' the runner countered. 'The Dutch are bringing in guns, troops, and more goods to trade for captives. They are more dangerous than the Portuguese, I think. I have come to give you the news, not argue with you. Do what you will, but I think I have earned your hospitality.'

Several of the older women clucked at this imputation on their manners and moved forward to take the guest to a hut where he could clean up and rest while they provided him with fresh clothes and prepared the evening's feast.

The runner stayed for a few days and then continued his journey north. There were many villages still to hear the news.

One evening, after training, Grandmother motioned Kisa, Kojo, and the twins to come to her hut. Yasuki came too. They sat in a circle, and Grandmother said, 'Soon you will be ready to fight. It is time for you to find the spirits that will help you on your journeys. We humans cannot conquer all the evil in the world without their help. Each of you must find your spirit animal. I have prepared a drink to help you this night. You will leave your bodies and enter into the spirits of animals. One that will stand out for you will be your guardian spirit. This spirit will stand by you for all of your life and help you.'

Saying this, she walked around the room and gave each a sip of a bitter-tasting brew in a brown wooden cup.

Kwame drank first and almost choked; it was so foul. Forewarned, Shani held her nose and swallowed fast. Kojo took his like a man, pretending it was sweet and making light of it.

At last it was Kisa's turn. There was half a cup left, and Grandmother said, 'Drink it all! You have the most to learn.' Kisa took the cup and looked hard at the liquid, wondering which ingredients were in it. 'I will show you tomorrow.' Grandmother read her mind again. 'Drink!'

She did not hurry. She held the cup to her lips and sipped it slowly, deliberately tasting it all as it slid like fire down her throat.

Grandmother led each of them to a separate part of the hut and gave them blankets to wrap their bodies in while their minds floated free. Kisa was already far above the Sentinel Tree as her body slid on to the mat.

She saw the night world with new eyes. Owl eyes. She was inside Great-Grandmother's totem, the spotted eagle owl. She felt the presence of Great-Grandmother riding with her. She felt her wings spread wide as she flew above the forest and out over the land. She could see the smallest animals in the forest and hear the tiny sounds they made with her powerful owl eyes and ears. All night long, she flew, and as the sun rose, she changed bodies. A great tawny eagle, Grandmother's totem, was rising up on the early morning thermals. Up and up he rose, and suddenly she was in his body, with Grandmother. Higher and higher they rose together, far higher than any owl could fly.

They flew so high that Kisa could see from ocean to ocean. 'See it all!' she heard Grandmother say. She could see beyond the forests to high mountains and on to the seas. She saw roads and villages and, far to the north, a city made of mud-brick buildings far larger than any village hut. On the ocean, she saw the white castles of the Europeans, built to enslave her people. And far to the east she saw her enemy, the Arab-Swahili trader and his band.

She swooped back down and over him, wanting to use her sharp claws to rip his eyes out. She was no longer in the eagle; she was in a large white-headed vulture instead. She found herself circling and circling, studying her enemy, learning everything she could about him, including his name. 'Mbwana Sefu,' she heard his lieutenant call out to him, and the name burned into her.

Suddenly she was called back to her body. She opened her eyes to find Grandmother offering her a drink of water. She gulped it down and sat up. She looked into Grandmother's eyes and knew that she knew everything because she had been there with Kisa for the whole journey.

Kojo, Shani, and Kwame were sitting by the fire, silent and reflective. Yasuki was watching them. Kisa and Grandmother joined them.

'Kojo, you start. What did you see?'

Kojo hesitated, looking for words. 'It is not like I was seeing. It was more feeling. I was inside my drum, and then I was in the tree that made my drum . . . and then I was in all trees, and they were speaking to me, telling me that they would help me through the drums.'

Grandmother nodded. 'Your power is in the language of the trees spoken through the drums. Call on them when you need to.'

Kwame spoke next. 'I was looking through the eyes of a grasshopper! Everything I saw, I saw many times—as if I was looking through a thousand eyes instead of two.'

Grandmother said, 'That is good. Grasshopper is small but important. When you need to be unseen but see all, then call on Grasshopper. He can go to places that you cannot.'

Then it was Shani's turn. 'I saw a herd of strange beasts, and then I was inside one looking out. They were tall, as tall as a tree, with long necks and the spots of the leopard. I did not know where I was.'

'You saw twiga, the giraffe! Giraffe is the wisest of animals because he does not talk. Only the foolish talk, talk, talk. Giraffe is fast too. With his long legs, he can run far, and with his long neck, he can see far too.'

Then Grandmother turned to Kisa. 'I saw your journey. Birds are your friends. Owl will give you the visions of the night, Eagle the visions of the day. But Vulture is most important. She will find your enemies unerringly. Death calls to her, and she finds it. Your enemies leave a trail of death behind them that Vulture can always find. And Vulture is the bravest of birds.

'Did you know that Udele the Vulture saved Mother Africa from the sun? Once, the sun was so close to the earth that it was burning us. The land was dry, and the plants could not grow. Only Vulture was brave and strong enough to fight with the sun. She pushed the sun back to where he journeys now. Vulture's head feathers were scorched by his heat, and they never grew back, but it was Vulture who saved us.'

Grandmother gave them healing cups of tea, and when their feet were back on the ground, she sent them home.

'I expected Kisa to be touched by more than one spirit guide,' she said over a cup of tea with Yasuki. 'But I did not know if the others would see anything. All have been touched by spirits. I will thank the Mother and the gods for the support they are giving our children.'

Yasuki, as usual, sat silent. Grandmother was comfortable with this. Yasuki always deferred to her knowledge, as she did to his. They were equals, and they knew it, though their areas of expertise were so different.

Far away in Agadez, having returned from Zanzibar with empty pockets, much to the disgust of his father, Sefu woke up from a new variation of his nightmare. Kisa came to him in animal form, a fierce eagle this time, and tried to kill him with her talons.

Enough, he thought as he huddled on his bed, heart racing. *I have to find her, use her, and then kill her.* Never mind the price she would undoubtedly fetch in either Zanzibar or the White Castle. She had to die. She was a witch. He had to kill her.

A few days later, during training, Yasuki called Kojo forward from the line of students and said, 'Today you may spar with me. To make the fight more equal, I will fight with my eyes closed.' Some of the younger students giggled at that. 'Silence!' Yasuki thundered then closed his eyes and, to prove he was serious, ceremoniously tied a cloth tightly around them. Then he waited for Kojo to attack.

Kojo bowed to his teacher, and to his surprise, Yasuki bowed back, though he could see nothing with his eyes. Then Kojo moved in and struck at Yasuki, who moved aside just enough for Kojo to miss his target. Kojo tried again with the same outcome.

Over and over, Kojo moved in and tried to punch or kick his teacher but never once did he come within a hand's reach of his target. Yasuki moved seamlessly, without any sense of hurry or effort. Suddenly his foot shot out and took Kojo's legs out from under him. Kojo fell hard, knocking the wind out of his lungs. 'Oof!' He got up as quickly as he could, only to have his legs knocked out again. This time he stayed down. Yasuki took off the blindfold, smiled, and bowed. Kojo jumped up and bowed back. The first fight was over, and there was no doubt in any of the students' minds that Yasuki did not need his eyes in order to see.

'You must practice sparring with your eyes closed. You must learn to use all of your senses, not just sight. You must hear every sound, feel every movement, feel the air move as your opponent moves, and hear his breathing and the sound of his feet on the ground. When you can fight blind, then you will reach a new level of ability.'

Now it was Kisa's turn to fight with Yasuki. As with Kojo, he fought her blindfolded, and she could not get in a blow. She stalked around him like the she-leopard, but there was no opening. Yet Yasuki was not able to take her legs out from under her. Like the cat, she saw every move he made and avoided it, if only by a whisker. On and on the fight went, neither landing a blow. At last, Yasuki stopped, and he took off the blindfold. 'You are quick and agile, my queen,' he said, calling her this for the first time in years. 'Your skills are growing. I am proud of you, my student, whom I could not touch. You will be a formidable foe to your enemies soon.'

'Only because of your training,' she said as she bowed back.

'And Grandmother's,' he reminded her.

The lesson ended, and Yasuki had the older students blindfold themselves when they fought. He admonished the younger students that their turn would come, and it was important that they never hurt the blindfolded students even if they could. 'I want you to show them that you can touch them but would never hurt them. You will have plenty of opportunities for that on the battlefields to come.'

The seasons came and went, and the training went on. Yasuki never seemed to be in a hurry, and yet he never let them get slack. They practiced every day except feast days and celebrations. He would stop for a wedding or a funeral; otherwise, whether it was pouring rain or hot and steaming, training went on. Serious illness was tolerated but not simple colds or aches and pains. Yasuki didn't care if the adults were too busy to train or the smaller children too tired, but he expected Kisa, Kojo, Kwame, and Shani to soldier on under all conditions.

At last, Yasuki pronounced their training complete. After declaring them samurai and ritually handing Kojo and the twins the weapons they had made, he turned to Kisa. He hadn't bowed before her since that first day eight years earlier, but he bowed now as he placed one of his samurai swords in her hands. 'Use it well, my queen,' he said as she accepted it.

Chapter 18

First Adventure

Kisa was restless. 'I'm eighteen years old! When can I fight?' Yasuki shook his head, and Grandmother laughed. 'You are not quite ready yet, but I think you must learn more about the world outside this village.'

'You have never seen the ocean. It's time you meet our neighbours—Ashanti, Ga, Fante, and Twi people. Go to the coast. See where our old village lies. Then go see the great slave fort, but do not get caught!

'After that, you and Kojo should go to Kumasi, capital of the Ashanti people. There you will meet people who hate slavery and others who profit from it. You can practice your arts, Kisa—disguise, sleight of hand, hypnosis—to fool those who see you.'

Kisa ran out to tell Kojo and the twins. Kojo was excited, but the twins were disappointed when she told them that they could not come. 'I am grown-up now! You are still children. When I was your age, I had to wait. Your time will come. Now it is my time . . . and Kojo's too, of course,' Kisa finished lamely when she realised that he wanted that acknowledgement.

There were several days of preparation before Grandmother would actually let them go. Kisa thought she repeated every lesson the old obeah woman had ever taught her and was a bit ill-mannered in her responses, muttering, 'Yes, yes, I know that already!' under her breath far too many times.

Kojo, on the other hand, listened intently and several times said, 'Oh, I forgot that. Thank you, Grandmother' or 'That is good to know,

Grandmother.' His politeness irritated Kisa too. She just wanted to get moving.

The night before they were to leave, Shani came shyly to Kisa, who was crouched on the floor of their hut, going through her travel kit one more time.

'Will you come outside, sister? We girls want to say goodbye to you and wish you good travels and a safe return.' Shani looked imploringly at her in a way that Kisa had never been able to resist.

'Yes,' she said, rising easily and walking out the door. Shani followed, and Kisa found herself in a circle of all the giggling girls of the village. They took her by her hands and pulled her across the village while chanting, 'Save her! Save her! They are going to marry her!' and laughing all the way.

Kisa couldn't figure out what they were talking about but went along with it. None of the adults were anywhere else to be seen. They took her in the special women's hut where women went for peace and quiet when they were having their bleeding time or just a place to sit with other women and talk and have cups of herbal tea without disturbance.

They set her down, and suddenly, out came the henna and the indigo. Shani and two of the other girls were playing with her hair, which was a shaggy mass of curls that had grown neck length over the years that she'd never cut.

'What are you doing?' Kisa said in-between her own laughter.

'We are preparing you for your journey, of course!' Shani answered. Kisa relaxed. She could see there was no way out, so she might as well enjoy herself.

The pampering was complete. Her sister and friends rubbed her feet and skin with oils. They combed and washed, plaited and hennaed her mane of hair and decorated her arms with henna and indigo patterns of strength and endurance. Then they dressed her in a fine indigo dyed dress and put bracelets on her arms. She protested against the dress and bracelets, but they told her there was going to be a feast and she had to look her best. Then Shani said, 'And the bracelets will protect your arms if you get into a fight, sister.' This was an idea which had not occurred to Kisa before, as jewellery had always seemed quite pointless to her.

'All right.' She gave in, and they finished their preparations. Suddenly, there was a knock at the doorway. Shani opened it, and Chief Abrafo was standing there. 'It is time,' he said mysteriously. 'Kisa, come with me.' It was an order, not a request, from the chief of her village, so she stood up. Led outside, she saw that a feast had indeed been prepared and all the village was gathered round the Sentinel Tree and the cook fires.

Chief Abrafo led Kisa to Grandmother and Kisa's mother, who were standing out the front, but she had eyes only for Kojo. He was dressed as finely as Kisa, but as a warrior . . . and a man about to be married. Next to him stood his sister; his foster mother, Esi; and Yasuki. All were dressed in their finest clothes, and every woman in the village was decked out in every piece of jewellery that they owned.

Kisa stopped and just stared, speechless for once. Kojo's foster father stepped forward and said, 'My son wishes to marry your daughter. He will pay the bride price. Do you agree?'

Chief Abrafo answered, 'As this woman has no father and I have been like a father to her, I will accept the bride price. Your son may marry my daughter.'

Grandmother stepped forward with Ama. They took Kisa by the hands, and Grandmother said, while Ama nodded, 'You will be married this day to Kojo. It is not seemly for you to travel together except as man and wife.'

Kisa started to protest, but her mother's hand covered her mouth. 'Hush, child. You know this must be done, and you know that you love him.'

Grandmother looked stern. 'You will not break my rule. You will not make any babies!' she whispered so that only the three of them could hear. Chief Abrafo hads stepped away from what was clearly women's business and out of respect for the old obeah woman. 'But you will be married!'

It was an order, and down deep, Kisa was surprised to realise that she was pleased about it. She loved Kojo, whatever the future brought to them. They were partners in this venture. He was her equal, whatever fate had in store for her. So when he stepped forward and offered her his hand, she accepted and walked with him to the sacred rock which was the altar to the old gods, where Chief Abrafo and Grandmother now stood facing them.

Chief Abrafo spoke first. 'These young people come to us in love and wish to be joined for life. They are about to embark on a journey of great peril for ones so young, and they do so to help us. These two warriors will be the leaders of the next generation of our tribe. They will be the defenders of our unborn children against the white devils. We will honour them before they go, and they will be joined in front of the gods and all who stand here tonight.'

He took their hands—Kojo's left and Kisa's right, which they had been holding—cut them each with his knife at the wrist, and tied them together with a cloth. 'Your blood is mingled now. You are one flesh and shall remain so to death.'

Grandmother stepped forward next. To Kojo she said, 'A man without a wife is like a garden without flowers.'

To Kisa she said, 'Marriage is the union of your male and female energies. Marriage is a journey through life which enriches our community. Marriage promotes sharing, tolerance, consideration, empathy, selflessness, and other virtues.'

Grandmother lit sacred herbs and blew the smoke on Kojo and Kisa to purify them and set the seal on their relationship.

The fetish priest then sealed the relationship with the ceremonial breaking of a kola nut into two halves and then binding them back together.

Kisa was in a daze, and the rest of the ceremony was hazy until Kojo touched his forehead to hers in front of the village. She scarcely heard the cheering and the applause as his forehead touched hers, and she felt an electric sensation in her groin, spreading out to the tips of her fingers and toes. The next thing she knew, the giggling girls were pulling her back and the men were moving in to congratulate Kojo.

Feasting followed, and then they were led to a new hut built specially for them and left alone for the night. Kisa suddenly felt shy again. She stood in her finery in the hut and looked down at the floor.

Kojo took her hand. 'You are my wife. I have loved you since the day I first saw you. You touched my heart, and I was yours forever. I know that we cannot make babies tonight, or perhaps forever, but you are my wife forever. The gods have given me all I ever wanted in life.' He took her other hand, and she looked up into his eyes.

'I will fight for you, someday die for you. To others you will be a sorceress and a warrior, but for me, you will always be my wife, and I will honour that first and always.' He put his arms around her, pulling her close to his body. She did not resist.

Quietly he whispered in her ear, 'The men have taught me what to do. You will feel such pleasure, my wife, as you have never known before, but I promise you that no new life will come out of this. Just give yourself to me now . . .'

And she did.

In Agadez, Sefu was planning to go west once more. He had woken from a particularly bad dream in which he was trying to capture Kisa. At first, he saw a girl child, and then she turned into an angry leopard with golden yellow eyes that chased him till he awoke in fear.

Enough! he thought. *I am going back to that village. I will take her, torture her, and then kill her and leave her body by the road for the vultures!*

He found Badru, Zuberi, and Kondo in the local whorehouse and told them to gather together a large party of mercenaries, much larger than normal.

'We are leaving the day before the Holy Day comes,' he told them gruffly. 'I want to go west again where the hunting is good. Prepare for a long journey!'

The next day, the whole village saw Kisa and Kojo off to the road that would take them south to the cape where their old village had once stood.

The journey through the forest to the coast was peaceful, and the pair met no other travellers. When they came at last to the ocean, they were amazed by the power and the noise of the waves beating on the rocky headland.

They could see the lighthouse of the Portuguese standing guard over the remains of the village. Kisa climbed a nearby hill to get a better look. She stood on a great granite boulder and gazed towards the sea and the first Portuguese structure she had ever seen. She felt Great-Grandmother's presence inside her, raised her fist in defiance, and spoke in a voice like Kojo had never heard before: 'You will not last! You will be gone from this land, and my people will return!'

A shiver went through him at the power in the words. It was a prophecy, of that he was sure.

She turned and strode south. He ran to catch up with her. 'Don't you want to explore your old village?'

'No! I do not wish to see the bones of the dead. I want to see the great castle. I will only return here when I can bring my people back.'

Two days' travel brought them to the castle. They could see it from a great distance because of its size and height. It was painted bright white and glittered in the sun. 'It's beautiful,' Kojo gasped.

'No, it isn't. The beauty is a lie. It is ugly,' Kisa said and spat on the ground in disgust.

She turned and faced the north. 'I don't want to go there yet. I want to look for allies in the fight. We won't find allies back there. Let's go to Kumasi. We will come back to this place when we can tear the walls down!'

Kojo was relieved. After the first view, the castle did feel evil. Like Kisa, he was not afraid, but it felt like a contamination on the land of Mother Africa. It was enough of a defilement just to look at it. He followed Kisa back to their campsite of the previous night.

The next day, Kisa and Kojo walked away from the ocean to the road that led to Kumasi, the capital of the Ashanti people, to learn about them and their involvement in the slave trade. Kumasi was a big town of many huts and compounds, surrounding a bustling marketplace and a great adobe building fit for the king of such an important tribe.

The marketplace was amazing to Kisa and Kojo, country villagers that they were. They were dazzled by the bright colours, not only of the clothing but of the large umbrellas that shaded the tables of the hawkers. The richer traders and businessmen had adobe rooms where their goods were displayed, with wooden doors that could be locked at night, though most traders lived at the back of their shops. All cooking, whether behind the shops or the huts, was done outside, so the air was filled with the smells of spicy soups and stews simmering in large black pots over small fires in every yard. Some of the spices were unfamiliar to Kisa, who only knew the local herbs, not strange powders from stranger lands.

The women wore bright dresses and turbans made from the kente cloth woven by their men. The woven mats over the hut doors were also bright, but the colour of the marketplace took their breath away. Suddenly they were in a magical kingdom of umbrellas and tables covered in the most amazing rainbow displays of gems, spices, gold, silver, and rolls of kente cloth and mats, all woven in bright colours with unique geometric patterns that added to the riot of patterns around them.

The noise levels were deafening too, as traders called out to new customers to draw them in and buyers bargained fiercely with sellers. In the noisy confusion, Kojo found it easy to shoplift small items while Kisa engaged the owners. They acquired the funds they needed to buy garments and jewellery suitable for a high-born lady and her man. She and Kojo sauntered around the town as a married couple, learning everything they could about this fierce, proud tribe.

They had a lot of guns and enough ammunition to waste it by shooting up into the air. Their women sported beautiful garments and fairly dripped with gold and silver bracelets, beads, and baubles. The upper class had slaves to serve them and do the chores.

'They won't join us against the Dutch,' Kisa said to Kojo. 'They get rich from the slave trade. Look at those guns!'

Sure enough, that afternoon, they watched a slave trader march into town from the road that went north to the market towns of Assino Manso and Salaga. Kojo watched in horror and Kisa in anger as a line of captives in chains were led through the town, guarded by ten or so black guards and led by a robed Arab-Swahili merchant in fine clothes and mounted on a horse.

Kojo spat on the ground as he passed. Kisa put her hand on his shoulder. They watched the line of miserable captives passed, and then they fell in behind them. The captives were taken to pens in the main marketplace to rest before the remainder of the journey to the coast and the great slave castle.

Kisa watched them for a moment and then turned and strode back north. 'Where are you going?' Kojo wanted to know as he followed her.

'Assino Manso and Salaga' was the answer. 'There is no point staying here. The Ashanti are profiting from the slave trade. They will not help us. I want to see the towns to the north. I want to see the slave markets, and I want to learn how to ride a horse!'

Kisa's tribe possessed no horses because they were forest-dwelling people. This forest was the home to the dreaded tsetse flies, which laid low both beasts and men with the sleeping sickness. But north of Kumasi, the land began to dry out, and by the time a traveller reached Tamale, the land was open grasslands and dotted with trees but not enclosed by them. Here, cattle flourished and men rode on horses.

Although the occasional rich slave trader would chance the life of his horse on the journey south, most animals were left behind in the northern villages and picked up again by the raiders for the long journeys either home or back to look for more victims and take more captives. Because of the sleeping sickness, the Akan people of Kumasi did not even use donkeys for carrying loads but used human porters instead. For this reason, the northern Dagomba and Gonja peoples called them Kanbongsie, meaning 'donkeys'.

'The Gonja people control Salaga. They obviously benefit from the slave trade too, but they also use horses and donkeys. I do not wish to be called a donkey, and I want to travel fast. Only a horse can do that. We have to be able to ride, Kojo.'

'But how will we pay for them?' Kojo, ever the cautious one, wanted to know.

'It is time to put our sleight-of-hand magic to work again, dear Kojo. We will steal it, of course! But from the slave traders. Let them finance their own destruction!'

They walked north for a day and reached Assino Manso. It was the final link in the key slave route from the north and had the largest slave market for merchants supplying slaves to the forts and castles on the coast. Kisa and Kojo wandered through it, seeing people newly washed in the Ndonko River nearby and now chained in the marketplace where they were being fed. 'Fattened up so they bring a higher price at the castles,' Kojo muttered. Kisa clenched her fists and walked on. 'I've seen enough. I don't suppose Salaga is any better, but let's go see.'

They walked for several more days, and the country became more wooded again as they approached the banks of the Volta River. This far from the sea, it was still narrow and shallow enough to ford without swimming, and on the other side was the market town of Salaga. It was as big as Kumasi and as busy, but the people were different. In Kumasi, the people were Ashanti, dark forest people. Here in Salaga, they met their first Gonja people. They were taller, and their brown skin was lighter with a red tint the colour of the sacred kola nut. The word *Gonja* meant 'kola nut' in the northern language of the older people there, the Dagomba tribes.

In the centre of Salaga, they found a bustling market where anything could be bought or sold: gold and precious metals, salt, all manner of spices and gems, food, clothing, and jewellery, as well as donkeys, horses, and slaves. The slave pens were just out of town. They were similar to the pens at Assino Manso.

Near the market was the palace of the head chief of the Gonja. It was a much larger mud-brick building than the huts of the villagers. The main difference from the southern town was the presence of corrals made of woven sticks in which the richer inhabitants kept horses and donkeys.

Kisa and Kojo spent several days wandering through the markets, using their pickpocketing skills to get the money they needed to buy two horses, saddles, and bridles. They chose their victims well, taking the money from slave traders and not the legitimate merchants.

After looking at the horses that were for sale, Kojo was sensible and chose a quiet animal. Kisa saw a half-wild Arab mare and had to have her. She had been watching others ride and was sure it would be easy. Kojo mounted first and soon had his quiet gelding moving left and right, but kick as he might, the horse refused to go faster than a walk.

Kisa tried to mount her mare, but she pulled away and refused to stand still. At last, Kisa had to curb her pride and ask Kojo to hold the mare's head till she could get mounted. As soon as Kojo let go, the mare took off, with Kisa hanging on for dear life. She hauled at the reins, but the mare was determined and had the bit in her teeth. Kojo mounted and followed, but his horse had no intention of catching the wild mare.

Finally, Kisa hauled hard on one rein, which turned her mare's head, and to Kisa's surprise, the mare slowed down and headed quietly back towards Kojo. When nose to nose, the horses stopped. 'I love her!' Kisa enthused in her excitement. 'I will call her Amara because she is so graceful.'

Kojo laughed. 'And my steed shall be known as Ayo because he is too happy to move fast and prefers to look at the scenery instead.'

Holding the reins tight, Kisa turned Amara's head north. Amara settled with Ayo close by and was now willing to walk. The trip to Salaga took a week, and the young couple enjoyed the journey. Kisa shed her female attire and travelled now like Kojo, as a warrior. The people they passed gave them a wide berth, intimidated as they were by sword-bearers on horses.

Enquiries were made as to where they came from, and they were pointed north again, to the road to Tamale. So after a few days' rest, they headed up the Tamale Road.

North of Salaga, the land grew drier, and the trees became smaller and less frequent. The land flattened out into a high plateau. There were few villages, and so they camped at night. They passed two slaving parties heading south, and they grieved at the condition of the captives, who looked half-starved and thirsty in the heat of the day. But there was nothing they could do.

'This is the road where we should start our war,' Kojo said after the second party passed them. 'They all come to the Salaga market, whether they come from the north-west, the north, or the north-east. They all have to funnel through here.'

'Then we need to look for a hidden place where we can camp and then strike.'

A half day's journey north of Salaga, they came across two low hills covered in trees. They rode their horses over the hill and found a small valley where they could hide while waiting for parties to come from the north.

Another two days brought them past several small villages, which were all built on the edges of creeks but with exposed country all around them. In each village, Kisa and Kojo talked with the residents to find out who was against the slave trade. Usually the chiefs were benefitting, but many of the villagers had lost loved ones and were against it. Kisa's magnetism attracted them, and several vowed to fight with her when they found out she intended to return with an army.

Continuing their journey, Kisa and Kojo reached the Pasa River, which offered good cover in the trees upstream but no good place for a camp.

'The slave masters have to let their captives drink here,' Kisa mused. 'Yes, it is another good place where we can ambush them.'

Travelling on the country became more and more open, with few hiding places and fewer creeks. In the villages of Chambulugu and Fuu, they saw strange small beehive-like buildings. Upon asking, they found they were called mosques. 'We are followers of the desert prophet,' the inhabitants told them. Kisa and Kojo were not sure what that meant and decided to ask Yasuki on their return home.

They came to the Mawi River next. The water was fresh and sweet but only flowing at a trickle, and the trees beside the stream were low and again would provide scant cover for a hunting party. North of the Mawi, the country was dry and open all the way to the crossroad town of Yendi. There were no good hiding spots along this section of the road.

'If we are going to hunt along the Salaga Road, we will have to do it right under the noses of the inhabitants of Salaga, it would seem. There is no place along here for a permanent camp,' Kojo concluded.

Yendi was an interesting town. The major road from the east passed through Yendi on the way to Tamale, and anyone going to Salaga had to go through Yendi as well. But it was not so much a trading town as the home of the head chief of the Dagomba people. The Dagomba were divided into many small communities throughout this country, and all had subchiefs. But all paid tribute to the head chief, the chief of chiefs, who had a palace in Yendi. Slavers passed through, but the locals disdained to have anything to do with them. Their business was the business of governing the Dagomba kingdom and negotiating with neighbouring peoples such as the Gonja.

They turned west, and a few days later reached Tamale. Like Yendi, it was built of mud bricks, and it had a mosque in the centre dedicated to the desert prophet. Kisa and Kojo felt out of place here and were getting homesick as well. They made enquiries and found that the slavers passed through here from all directions, going west to Wa, east to Yendi, south to Salaga, and north to Bolgatanga.

'The Salaga Road still looks like one of the best places to attack slavers,' Kojo said, and Kisa nodded. 'There are fewer people living there, and there are those small hills where we can watch and hide. The slavers have to stop at small streams that cross the road so their captives can drink. Those are the best places we have seen where we could lie in ambush. It's just too open up here.'

Kisa agreed. 'Between Salaga and Assino Manso, the bush is too thick and there is more water, so there is no guarantee where they will stop. And too many villages too. I think we should go back now and tell Sensei what we have found. The Salaga Road is where we can go to war!'

The next day they turned south, and that was when they noticed a line of rocky hills to the west. 'That is a place we should have a closer look at. From there, we could see what is happening on the northern roads,' Kisa remarked.

Chapter 19

On the Wings of Udele

When they reached the escarpment, they climbed to the highest point, where they could see far in all directions. To the east lay Dagoba and Tamale. To the west was endless savannah woodland through which sparkling blue rivers ran. Back to the south, they could see the White Volta River flowing towards Tamale Port. And north beyond the escarpment they could just make out heat waves rising off the distant desert.

Kisa saw vultures in the sky and yearned to join them, to see further, and suddenly, to her surprise, she was looking out of a great vulture's eyes. Always before, she had to use Grandmother's potion to make the leap, but today it seemed as easy as taking a leap on to her horse. She was a great white-headed vulture, the matriarch of her clan. 'Udele.' Kisa felt rather than heard the name. 'I will serve you, sorceress . . .'

On the great wings of Udele, she soared higher and higher. With Udele's keen eyes, she spotted a great road running straight and true from west to east. On it there was a caravan of donkeys moving slowly but relentlessly to the east. Kisa flew over the road and then circled lazily over the donkeys and their loads. The caravan was led by an Arab on a horse. Behind him were guards and slaves, leading the donkeys who were bearing great loads. Covered as they were, Kisa could only guess at their contents.

At last she returned to the escarpment and mentally dismounted into her waiting body, asleep in Kojo's arms. Kojo greeted her with a grin and a touch of his forehead to hers. 'You went quick.' He laughed. 'My arms were growing weak with your weight.'

Kisa laughed back. 'I do not think so. You are stronger than that!' Then she told him how easy it had been and about seeing the caravan in the distance.

'I found myself in a great she-vulture, one with a white head. She is called Udele, and she is the mother of her tribe. She gave me her allegiance and said she would take me anywhere I wanted to go. We flew over the road to Wa, and I saw a caravan!

'There were slaves in that caravan, but I do not think they were new captives. And I could not tell what the donkeys carried.

'Then I soared higher, and I saw something so amazing I have trouble with the words, Kojo. I will draw it for you.' She found a place with loose dirt and began drawing her first map with a stick. 'This line is these hills and rocks. This *X* is where Tamale is. This line is the road going north of Tamale. From a great height, I could see all the way to a river, many days' walk north, and there I saw a city far greater than anything we have so far. All the villages and towns put together would be nothing in this place! There were temples and houses, not huts, and compounds covering the banks of the river for as far as I could see, and that was very, very far! And so many caravans coming and going! Many of the slave masters come down that road to Tamale.

'Far to the west, I saw the sea, and far to the north, I saw the desert, but not what lay beyond them. To the west and south, I saw the forests that cover our Mother, and they too went as far as I could see.' She faltered. 'It is hard to explain. I wish I could take you with me to see it too.'

Kojo smiled and held her by the arm. 'I love it that you can see all of this. I am content to hear of it from you. It is the spirit of the drums that I see. We have to see different things, my love.'

'It would still be easier to show you! Oh, Kojo, the Mother is so big! She goes on forever in three directions. Only the sea stops her. Our village is so small. It's all so much bigger than we are. What can we hope to do?'

Kojo was surprised. He had never seen doubt on Kisa's face before. 'If the Mother is so great, then she is greater than all our enemies. She knows we fight for her children. She has sent you to defend them from the evil ones. She does not love them for what they do. She needs us to fight them. And if we lose, it will not matter. We must do this for your father, for my family. It is as Sensei Yasuki has taught us. Death does not matter. We must face it and fight. And if we do that, we will win! I am sure of it. I am sure of you, Kisa, my wife, my lover, my . . . queen.' Kojo stopped, embarrassed, but then he saw the glow return to her eyes.

'With you beside me, my warrior husband, I cannot lose,' she whispered. 'You give me strength. I will not doubt again. But I have seen how many slave masters and traders there are. We must get home. We must first of all protect our own. Then we will work out a way to take the war to the slave masters.'

They left the escarpment and, hand in hand, descended to the valley below, and next day they left for home.

Halfway home, they came to the village of Kintampo that was still in open country, but ahead they could see the gathering forest. 'We cannot take the horses home with us, but I want them again when we come north. Let's find a farmer who will keep them for us—for a price, of course.' Kisa checked her money pouch. There was more than enough stolen from the various market towns to pay a farmer handsomely to look after the animals.

That done, they walked for another week until they were back in their own country. It was good to be home, and from the excited greetings of the villagers, they had been missed.

Grandmother, Yasuki, and the chief greeted them first, and there was a great feast that night in honour of their return. Then life slid back into a normal pattern. Kisa and Kojo went back to training, and Kisa assisted Grandmother with their obeah roles. Moons waxed and waned, and then life changed again forever.

Chapter 20

Sefu Meets his Match

Mbwana Sefu woke in a sweat. This time she killed him! He couldn't remember that happening before, but he had been lying beneath her, choking in his own blood just before he woke. He had to find that girl and kill her. He did not want to be haunted by a mere woman for the rest of his life. There was no other way. He had to find that village again and soon.

He'd been on the road for two weeks already. He drove his raiders past villages that he could have raided but did not. The raiders grumbled, but all they earned for their troubles were beatings. For Sefu, there was only one village that mattered now. Once she was dead, he could concentrate again on making money.

The village had been moved again, deeper into the forest, but such a large group of people could not move far. A few extra days were needed, but at last Sefu spotted the signs and knew he was close: a broken pot, brambles across the paths, and in the distance a wisp of smoke from a cooking fire.

Sefu drove his men forward. There was no one in the big tree this time. He was disappointed. He wanted to see her again in that tree, a grown woman now and ripe for taking, but the tree was empty. He wanted to see her in a real female body, not a monster in his dreams. A stab of fear suddenly struck him. *She knows I am coming.* Potential captives had never struck fear in him before. He pushed the thought aside and rode forward.

The raiders heard drums in front of them. They were getting close, and the villagers knew they were coming.

Sefu pushed through the site of the old village. He could see that they'd moved deeper into the jungle, but he had no doubt he would find them.

The track was narrow, and the raiders were forced to walk single file. Suddenly, in front of him, Sefu saw a strange sight: a black man dressed in strange black-and-white clothing and holding two swords. 'Begone!' the man cried out. 'Or you will die here!' And as he said this, arrows came from all directions, felling five of the raiders and leaving three more screaming in pain.

Sefu kicked his horse and tried to ride the man down, but Yasuki stepped deftly to one side and drove his sword into Sefu's leg. Sefu roared with pain and anger. 'Attack!' he screamed. 'Attack!'

The raiders were not used to this kind of resistance, but the lieutenants Zuberi and Kondo hit them with their whips and drove them forward. They came into a clearing and faced thirty villagers armed not just with farming implements but swords. At the head was a beautiful young woman. Sefu recognised her and pulled his horse up so hard that he reared high in the air. His men closed in around him.

The villagers closed in too, led by Kisa, Kojo, and Yasuki, swords swinging. Kisa was heading for Sefu, determined to kill him, but the raiders closed in around him. She struck hard at the head of the first raider she met.

Kojo and Yasuki were just as deadly. The raiders fell back, but Badru used his horse to ride around behind the defenders. He saw a lone woman watching the battle. It was Kojo's sister, Afia.

Too late Afia saw the scarred, ruined face of Badru. She quailed in fear at the sight then turned to run, but his horse was faster. As he galloped past, he grabbed her and pulled her over his horse's neck. Turning, he raced around the huts and back to the raiding party, who were now fighting for their lives.

Sefu rode forward to fight with Kisa, whom he intended to disarm and capture. He was very sure of himself, with thirty hardened raiders behind him and his sword firmly in his big right hand. He was much larger than Kisa in weight and height, and he was mounted. A paunch was developing around his waistline, but his arms were thick with muscle. He had been a slaver for years. He'd fought in many one-sided battles against peaceful unarmed villagers. He thought these people were no different, even though they were armed with spears, swords, and bows instead of just farming tools.

He pulled his horse up into a rear to frighten Kisa. A wave of arrows flew from her bowmen into the black stallion's chest. As he was still rearing, she raced in with a spear in her left hand and a long slim samurai sword in the other. She plunged the spear into the horse's heart then stepped out of the way as it fell.

Sefu faced Kisa. She stood before him with that slim and puny-looking sword in her right hand, but it was the look in her eyes that caused him to step back. He felt again the sharp stab of fear he had felt in his dreams night after endless night.

He lifted his great sword and, grasping it two-handed, stepped in to kill her. He thought that when Kisa lifted her sword to him, he could just knock it from her hand and cleave her head open, as she had just done to his man.

She stepped forward to meet him. He swung his sword, and she met it with hers. He was surprised at her strength. He expected her sword to fly out of her hand, but it didn't. He swung again, and she parried the blow easily, cutting him on the wrist. It surprised him so much that he took two steps backwards, his wounded arm throbbing.

Kisa came at him slashing. Her eyes suddenly looked like the leopard in his dreams. The fear he felt caused him to lose his balance on a backward step, and he fell down. Kisa leaped towards him, ready to kill him at last. His raiders were busy fighting Kojo, Yasuki, and the villagers. He was hers! Sefu crawled backwards, desperately parrying her sword with his.

Badru rode up just as Kisa was beating her enemy to the ground with stroke after stroke. He watched his older brother's sword falter. He heard him beg for mercy. 'Please! No!'

It was cut short by the samurai sword slicing through Sefu's throat. He fell, gurgling and gasping as his life's blood slowly bubbled out of him. Kisa stood above him, splattered in his blood.

At that moment, Kojo saw his sister on Badru's horse and cried out, 'Afia!'

Badru wasted no time. He turned and raced back to the path that led out of this deadly village. As he rode, he called to the only two other men on horseback, Zuberi and Kondo, to follow him. They took one look at the armed and angry villagers and their leader lying dead at the feet of the female warrior, and they changed their allegiance. Dashing off after Badru and Afia, they left the rest of the raiders to die.

Kojo and Kisa could not reach the horsemen without finishing the raiders first. Kisa's white-hot anger rose in her like a volcano. 'Die!' she screamed, and her call was taken up by Yasuki on one side and Kojo on the other. Addy began beating his drum as Chief Abrafo and all the armed villagers rushed to help their leaders.

Kisa and Kojo had prepared for this battle for seven years, and now their hatred was unleashed. They cut a swathe through the raiding party, slaughtering all in their path. Soon all but three of their enemies lay dead around them. The last raiders threw down their weapons and begged for mercy, but they were cut short by Kisa's sword.

Kojo tried to stop her, but she was fast and deadly, shaking off the touch of his hand and finishing the job. Yasuki leaned on his sword and shook his head. 'Do not become like them, my queen,' he said, loud enough for her to hear when she was lifting her sword to hew them again.

She stopped midblow, her chest heaving. All fell silent. Then someone raised a cheer. 'Kisa!' And the rest took it up. 'Kisa, Kisa, Kisa!' The drum kept the rhythm. Then someone else called out, 'Obeah!' and the drum and voices took that call up.

Kisa kept her samurai sword raised as she dug the tip of the machete into the dirt. Her left hand went up in a fist. She lowered her sword arm but left her fist held high as the villagers chanted her name and her rank over and over.

Her breathing calmed. She felt an overwhelming sense of sadness. She stared at the bodies—not just the raiders but several villagers who had fallen too. She lowered her fist. Tears welled in her eyes, but she blinked them back, determined to stay strong. Kojo was by her side, Yasuki too, and Grandmother was walking up to join them.

Chief Abrafo called for silence. Addy stopped drumming and took the voices with him.

'We are victorious,' Chief Abrafo said quietly and yet loud enough for all who lived to hear. 'We owe it to you. We will stand by you as you have stood for us.'

Kisa had been drowning in her own thoughts through all this. Her attention had turned back to the body of Sefu. Why did she not feel triumph? Why was his death such a hollow victory? She looked in the direction where Badru had ridden off with Afia. Killing Sefu ended nothing. A new enemy was even now riding off with someone she loved, someone she would never see again. *No!* her mind screamed.

Then Chief Abrafo knelt before her.

She looked at him, not understanding for a moment the significance of what he was doing. Confused, she did not know what to do.

Suddenly Yasuki and Grandmother appeared beside the chief. Yasuki spoke first.

'Today you have become a warrior.'

He paused then pulled his second samurai sword from its scabbard. Kneeling, he presented it to her.

'May it serve you well, my queen.'

In a trance, Kisa accepted it.

Then Grandmother spoke, 'I can teach you no more, sorceress.'

She held out a jet-black stone, an amulet on a leather thong.

'Hold this stone, and you will connect with the Mother herself.'

The old obeah woman put the stone in Kisa's hand and folded her gnarled hands around it.

'Feel her strength pour into you . . .'

A surge of power, like a bolt of lightning, ran through Kisa. Through their now transparent hands, she saw the stone glowing bright yellow.

No one in the village moved or breathed.

Grandmother removed her hands and stood back.

Suddenly she knelt before Kisa, going down heavily on one knee.

'You are the sorceress now. I pass the power of obeah to you.'

Rising again, the old woman turned to the villagers.

'Behold the sorceress!'

Leaping to his feet, Chief Abrafo took up the call, which was echoed by all.

'Behold the sorceress!'

Kojo grabbed his drum and began a beat in time.

'Kisa! Kisa the sorceress! Kisa the warrior! Kisa! Kisa! Kisa!'

Kisa turned to her people, seeing them as if for the first time. She raised her clenched fist high.

'Somunye!' she shouted above all the voices, and silence fell at the sound of the word that meant 'we are one'.

'Somunye,' she repeated, softer but stronger.

'Somunye,' they answered, softly at first, and then it became a chant, echoed by Kojo's drum.

Wild with the ecstasy of victory, they danced, chanting 'Somunye, somunye, somunye!' around Kisa, who stood stock-still, saluting them.

Then they lifted her in triumph and carried her back to the village.

CHAPTER 21

The War Begins

All the villagers wanted to do was celebrate their victory, but it was hollow for Kisa and Kojo. As soon as they could break free from the singing and dancing, they strode up to Grandmother and Yasuki.

'We are going after Afia,' Kisa began.

'Of course you are,' Grandmother agreed.

Yasuki nodded. 'Take some supplies. Go swiftly, for they are on horseback.'

Grandmother took Kisa's hands and looked deep in her eyes. Kisa felt love pass through those hands to every part of her being.

'We will look after everyone here,'Grandmother said.

'When you return, you will have a small army prepared for the war that you began this day.'

Kojo stepped forward. He bowed to his teachers and thanked them. Then he turned to Kisa, urgent with his fear for Afia.

'Come, my love. Afia needs us.'

They took a few minutes to pack food and water for the journey, then they set off on foot after the slavers.

The war had begun.

Timeline

Some of the world's great civilisations flourished in Africa before 1400, including Kush, Axum, Mali, and Great Zimbabwe. In this early period, Africans participated in extensive international trading networks and in trans-oceanic travel. Some African states established trading relations with India, China, and other parts of Asia before these were disrupted by European intervention.

AD 800	North Africa is invaded by successive waves of Muslims from the east. Indigenous people in these areas either converted or moved south.
1200–1400	Gold from the great empires of West Africa, such as Ghana, Mali, and Songhai, helped power the economies of Europe at this time. Including the lure of spices in the east, the wealth of West Africa, especially as a source of gold, encouraged the voyages of early European explorers.
1400s	The Spanish and Portuguese explore the Atlantic coast of Africa and begin cultivating sugar on the Atlantic islands of the Canaries, Cape Verde, and Madeira. As this became both successful and labour-intensive, the first captives were brought from the Congo to do the work.
1472	The Portuguese start building a trading fort in West Africa at Axim (in modern Ghana).
1482	Christopher Columbus visits Axim. The Portuguese build Elmina Castle at Cape Coast (Ghana).
1492	Columbus 'discovers' the Americas but thinks it's India.

1493	Columbus takes sugar cane from the island of Hispaniola in the New World.
1500s	The Spanish and Portuguese develop sugar plantations in the Caribbean and Brazil. Attempts to use native people as slaves largely failed, and the Atlantic slave trade began.
	Kisa's people move their village from the coast to the forest. Grandmother is a child at the time.
	Yasuki is taken to Japan and becomes a samurai.
	Grandmother becomes the village obeah.
1600	Sefu is born.
1616	Kojo is born.
1619	Kisa is born.
1622	Kisa climbs the Sentinel Tree.
1624	Sefu raids Afia and Kojo's village.
1625	Twins are born. Kisa is six, Kojo nine.
1627	Sefu finds the village in the maze for the first time.
1631	Kisa is twelve, Kojo is fifteen, and the twins are six. Raiders come back and take Kisa's father.
1633	Yasuki arrives and training begins. Kisa is fourteen, Kojo sixteen.
1637	The Dutch take Elmina Castle from the Portuguese.
	Kisa becomes the sorceress.

CPSIA information can be obtained
at www.ICGtesting.com
Printed in the USA
FSHW011953121118
53748FS